HERB'S FIRST 100 YEARS

&

The Book of Truths

by Randy Perkins

Published in the United States by Pinsker Publishing

ISBN: 1-4116-3911-1

First Edition: September 2005

10 9 8 7 6 5 4 3 2 1

http://geocities.com/perkins_r_k/
http://www.lulu.com/perkins

Pp Pinsker Publishing

This story is dedicated to everyone I have ever known.

You know who you are.

Thank you.

Sunday, December 8th, 1996

Truth #122
Every person's life is a work in progress,
shaped every moment by the things they think, say, and do

If you ever find yourself at Denver's airport around sunrise, look west and witness a sight often pleasing to the eye. On most days you will see a handful of snow-crested peaks reaching tall into the thin, mile-high air. Just ahead of sunrise, as darkness is chased west, a wave of cold air runs brisk across the landscape bringing a crispness invigorating to both skin and lungs. The sun crests the flat eastern horizon and the mountains are bathed in a reddish-pink glow.

As I watched this sight come to light, a familiar voice rolled passed my ears calling a question from behind. "Are you on time, Randy?"

I turned to find Samuel Sampson pulling a luggage cart. They moved as if attached, a tool in the hand of its master. A carpenter has his hammer, a surgeon his scalpel, a painter his brush. Sam has his luggage cart and loaded or empty, it always seems to move for him in an effortless glide. "Van is due any minute," I replied.

"New York, New York," he said ruffling through a stack of airline luggage tags as if it was a deck of cards. "You know, they're buildin' a replica in Las Vegas. S'pose-to-be quite the place. I get to Vegas pretty often. When I hit a big payoff, maybe then I'll take some money and visit the real one."

1

Sam is a skycap; a man experienced with the intricacies of moving luggage from city to city, country to country... He has always been quick to provide me a much needed and always appreciated helping hand.

"How many times you been to New York, Randy?"

"A few dozen, I guess. You've never been?"

"Juss-cuz I work at the airport don't mean I ever get to go anywhere. And when I do go somewhere, Vegas is the place for me."

"You should try one of our tours. Take your wife on vacation. I'll see you get a discount on the trip."

"I appreciate that, Randy. I really do. But I don't think we're quite ready for one of your tours yet. Seems to me like all your people are... Pardon me for putting it this way but they're..."

"Old?" I replied for him. We were both chuckling as my cell phone rang. Answering, I listened to an update from a dispatcher then answered, "Tell your driver I'm on Level Five, Door 506."

"Close?" Sam asked.

"Five minutes. " I replied as I adjusted my tie, put a mint in my mouth and flexed the corners of my lips hoping to set my expression in some fashion of a pleasant grin.

"You ever get tired of doin' this? I mean, it seems to me you travel a lot."

"Do you ever get tired of moving your cart?"

Sam answered, "I see what you mean."

"I must tell you though, this trip is something special. There is no place like New York City."

"What-do-ya-do when ya get there?"

"Visit the sights, eat in the restaurants, see a few shows, and make sure the ladies have adequate opportunities to shop. It's a busy trip. There won't be any free time for me. If I'm not with the group showing them the sights, then I'm on the phone with vendors or checking in with the office. There is always something I need to do."

2

"How many years you been a tour guide?"

"Four years. Almost five."

Before long, the van appeared at the end of the causeway. Sam stepped out onto the pavement and waved an arm in an attempt to signal the driver where we were. Upon seeing Sam, the driver sped up, steered toward us and with an alarming lack of precision, brought the vehicle to a stop. Stepping up, I opened the sliding door of the van and was immediately struck by the looks on all but one of the faces.

"Good morning," I said to the twelve people. "My name is Randy Perkins and I will be your guide for the next six days." Some of them were frighteningly pale.

"Sir," the woman nearest me said in a cross, anger-filled tone, "did you have anything to do with hiring this driver?"

"What's wrong?" I asked.

Comments erupted from the group in a cadence of resentment and fear. "DOES HE HAVE A DRIVERS LICENSE? - HE MIGHT HAVE KILLED US. HE SCARED ME NEAR TO DEATH! – I'LL BE CALLING A CAB ON OUR RETURN." This was not a good way to start my tour.

As I tried to process the comments my eyes moved from face to face and came to rest upon a man sitting in the far corner of the back row. A broad smile creased the wrinkled skin of his cheeks. He was the only member of the group who seemed unperturbed by the ride. Upon eye contact, he let his head bob with a nearly imperceptible acknowledging nod.

"I'm sorry folks. Please accept my apologies and rest assured we will be taking action to correct whatever has happened here. Your safety is of utmost importance and fear should never be a part of your tour." I cast my eye to the driver's seat and wondered where the man had gone.

"He should lose his license!" the woman nearest me reiterated pointing at the empty seat. Other passengers nodded to agree.

"If you will all gather inside the double doors, you'll find an area where you can sit and relax for a few minutes." I pointed and repeated, "Inside the door and to the right. Restrooms are located a short walk down the lobby. In a few minutes, we will all need to check in with a representative from the airline. After that you can start making your way to the gate.

"What gate are we leaving from?" a woman asked.

"B-10, but you need to see the ticket agent and check in before you go anywhere."

"Where do we do that?" someone else asked.

"Here," I repeated. "An agent is on her way and we have arranged a special check-in that will happen in the waiting area just inside the double doors."

"What airline are we flying?" another queried.

"What about my bags?" still another chimed in.

One by one, I answered their questions and offered the women a helping hand as they stepped out of the van. The last person off was the calm, smiling gentleman. As he twisted and sidestepped his way around the other seats, he shifted an ivory-handled collapsible cane and a brown leather folio from hand to hand.

"Can I help you with those?"

"Thank you ," he said handing me his things. His cane was light as a feather. The folio felt like it contained the Denver telephone book.

"This is the hardest part of our journey," I said, "getting in and out of the van."

His smile grew slightly wider as he set his feet on the pavement and straightened. "Herb Conroy," he introduced himself, took his things and extended his hand.

"Good to know you, Herb. Randy Perkins." I shook his hand.

Herb looked to be a man in his early to mid-eighties. Tall and thin, he had a strong handshake but a very bony hand. His clothes were vintage 1960s - gray slacks, gray sport coat and a matching Landry hat. Hazel eyes were bright and alert. He had a slight bend and unnatural flat spot in the bridge of his nose. It looked to me like it had been broken more than once. With a

4

flick of his wrist, Herb extended his cane. Folio tucked under an arm, he adjusted his hat and made his way inside.

All of the group looked to be in their late seventies or older and in spite of the problems with getting them to the airport, all seemed healthy, alert, and mobile. It's not a good thing when the first person associated with your company makes full use of an opportunity to frighten or piss off your passengers. I turned my attentions to the back of the vehicle where I expected to find Sam and the driver unloading luggage. Instead, I found the man kneeling on a rug on the sidewalk, bowing and chanting. Sam looked at me and shrugged.

"Excuse me," I said. "It's time to unload luggage."

"Can't you see I'm praying?" he replied.

"Yes, I can. It would also appear my passengers had to say a few prayers on the way in this morning." The man continued to chant and bow. "I've never seen a group more frightened by a ride." He looked up but continued to bow.

Sam read my frustration and moved with me to the back door of the van. "What religion you s'pose he's practicing?" he asked as I opened the door and handed him a suitcase.

"Why?"

"He's facin' west. Don't know of any religions who pray to the west."

"Salt Lake City is west of here. Maybe he is Mormon."

"More like a moron," Sam replied as he started to tag the bags.

Just as I finished pulling the last suitcase, the driver appeared rug in hand. "What's your name?" I asked.

"What's it to you?"

"It's everything to me. I think I'm safe in saying, you won't be driving for us again."

"Screw you, shithead," he eloquently replied. "Pay me and I will be on my way."

"You'll have to see your boss for your paycheck."

"LISTEN UP," he barked as he poked his index finger at my chest stopping just short of contact. "The only reason I'm up at

5

dawn carting these old bastards around is 'cause I was told there would be cash for me when I dropped them off. Hand it over."

Sam moved around behind the man and winked at me as if to say he was ready to help, but I shook him off and pulled an envelope out of my coat pocket that contained a $50 gratuity in cash.

"See ya," he said snatching it from my hand. With a cocky strut, he made his way back to the driver's seat.

"Good help is hard to find, Randy," Sam said.

"Yes it is," I replied. "Yes it is."

With the luggage tagged and on its way, I gave Sam two $20s, thanked him, and reminded him of when we were scheduled to be back. "You have my cell number?" he asked.

I nodded, " I will call you if anything changes or we are late."

Inside, I again greeted my dozen travelers. "Folks, welcome to Denver International Airport. Please let me apologize again for this morning's ride. Let's not let this unfortunate incident get in the way of your vacation." Most of them bobbed their heads in agreement. "The first thing we need to do is check in with the airline. In a minute, a representative will be down to ask security questions and look at your ID's. After that, feel free to make your way to the gate. Or if you'd rather walk with me, I'll be heading that way just as soon as we are done here."

"Where are our bags?" one of the ladies asked.

"The skycap has them and is checking them through to Newark."

"When will I see it again?"

"It will be delivered to your room at the hotel in Manhattan."

"When do I get my ticket?"

"I will give you your boarding ..."

Check-in was uneventful. The ticket agent from the airline arrived and asked her questions and checked ID's. I used the opportunity to mingle with my passengers, pass out packets of information, and get a feel for the group. Three of them had traveled with the company before, but none of them had traveled with me. After clearing security, an underground shuttle whisked us to our concourse. From there, it was a short walk to the gate. With everyone accounted for, I passed out boarding passes and tried to connect faces with names. "I'm sorry, you are?"

"Theda McCraken," the woman replied. "But I would prefer that you call me Rose."

I thumbed through my stack of tickets. "Ever been to New York, Rose?" From the corner of my eye I noticed the lady sitting next to her roll her eyes.

"Yes, but it was years ago. My husband, Frank, he's been dead for 20 years now, we went to New York for our honeymoon."

"What year would that have been?"

"1945."

"Wow. I can safely say the city has changed a lot since then. What do you remember most about New York in 1945?"

"Well I guess what I remember most was the war. Frank was wounded fighting in Italy. When he was well enough to come home, the first thing we did was get married. Everything seemed so uncertain. We didn't know what was going to happen from one day to the next. Well Frank had seen New York before he was shipped to Europe, but he didn't get to spend any time there and when we talked about a honeymoon, he asked if it was someplace I wanted to see. We had a wonderful time. And for me, the biggest city I had seen before that was Denver. Denver wasn't very big back then. It was a small city compared to New York in 1945. It was so exciting." She paused for a moment and then said, "I know now what I remember most about New York in 1945. I remember being in love."

Theda Rose McCracken seemed as gentle and pleasant as a person could be. "And I'm guessing you would be Fanny Hosack," I said to the woman seated next to Rose. Fanny was the woman most vocal about the recklessness of the driver of the van. Rose and Fanny would be sharing a room.

"Yes, I am."

"Ever been to New York, Fanny?"

"Oh yes, several times. Tell me Randy, is there any chance we could be upgraded to first class. I see you have tucked us in the back of the airplane. Considering the price we paid for this trip, I was sure we would be flying first class."

"I'm sorry, Fanny, we might be able to get you moved to a different seat, but none of us are flying first class."

"I have a medical condition. I really need the extra room."

Fanny also had a terrible case of bad breath – as sour as rancid milk. "And what would that condition be?" I asked stepping back in search of fresh air.

"My ankles swell," she said in a near whisper.

I looked down at Fanny's ankles. "What would you like me to do for you?"

Rose interrupted, "Oh it's all right. We'll be okay, won't we Fanny?"

"Could you at least try to get us upgraded to first class?"

'That's too much trouble, Fanny." Rose protested. "Don't be a pest."

"If no one is using those seats, why shouldn't we make use of them? Good God Rose, it does not hurt anyone to ask."

"Ladies," I offered, "let me see what I can do."

Before attending to Fanny's request, I continued to hand out boarding passes and ended up with two in my hand. I scanned the waiting area for Herb Conroy but didn't see him anywhere. "Virginia Crawford," I called and scanned for an acknowledgment. "Virginia Crawford," I called again. As far away as our seating area allowed, a hand halfheartedly lifted above the owner's head. The woman squirmed a bit in her chair as I approached. "Mrs. Crawford, how nice it is to meet you." I handed her a boarding pass and took note that she was unusually tense. Apprehension seemed to emanate from her pores. "Are you all right?"

She shook her head no. "I'm having second thoughts about this trip."

"Can I ask why?" I sat in an empty chair next to her.

"I'm thinking now I've bitten off more than I can chew. You see, I've never flown. I know it's silly. I bet I'm the only person in Colorado who hasn't flown. I always knew it would bother me, but I didn't think I would be shivering in my shoes. Maybe it was our ride to the airport. Am I'm overreacting? I don't know what to do. Could you please tell me what to do?"

"What do you think would happen if you were to get on this airplane?"

"I suppose I'm worried it could crash."

"Yes, I suppose it could. But you know, you could have crashed on the way to the airport this morning. In fact, that is much more likely to happen than crashing in an airplane, Mrs. Crawford,"

"Please call me Ginny."

"Ginny, if you don't feel comfortable getting on this airplane, then you shouldn't."

"But I really want to see New York."

"Then come."

"I'm worried I might panic."

"Do you panic?"

"Only since my husband died."

Visualizing Ginny in a panic on the airplane, all kinds of unpleasant images came to mind. Ginny passing out from trepidation - Ginny having a heart attack - Ginny pacing the aisle like a caged animal - Ginny frantic with fear... The scenarios went on and on. "Maybe it would be best if you stayed behind." I suggested.

"You won't take me?"

"It doesn't sound like you are able to go."

"I think I could be all right."

"You think?"

"I just don't know what to do. Tell me what to do and it will be okay."

If ever in my life I had witnessed despair, it was at that moment looking at Ginny's face. She sat back in her chair unsure, full of fear, and on the verge of tears. "I'm sorry, Ginny, I can't tell you what to do."

"Come with us," came the voice of Herb Conroy from over my shoulder. The tone carried an assurance comforting to even me. He crouched clutching his leather folio under his left arm and leaned in on his cane. "It's going to be quite the journey. The Big Apple. Gotham. Possibly, the greatest city on earth. Every street has a story to tell. Every corner will seem familiar or remind you of something - a movie - a song. Times Square, the Empire State Building, Wall Street, the United Nations, the Metropolitan Museum of Art, Broadway shows and fancy restaurants. Isn't that why you signed up for this trip, to see those things and to stand on the streets of Manhattan?"

"Yes, that's exactly why I signed up."

"Then this is your chance. Come with us."

It was easy for Herb to tell Ginny to come along. He would not be responsible for her if she should freak.

"What do you say, Randy? Don't you think Ginny should see New York City?"

"Absolutely. But I also think Ginny knows better than anyone whether or not she will be comfortable on the airplane."

"Could I sit with one of you?"

Herb looked to me and replied with the same, comforting tone, "I'm sure Randy can arrange most anything." His grin widened as if to playfully challenge me.

I said, "Let me see what I can do."

Truth #43
Life is an adventure

With a little help from the agent at the gate, I managed to get Ginny, Herb and I all seated together. I figured since Herb had convinced the worrisome woman to come along, it might be helpful to have him close should the need arise to help keep her calm. Besides, I liked the man right off; there was something about him that was easy to be around. The three of us sat with

Ginny in the middle, Herb in the window seat with me on the aisle. The rest of my passengers were scattered throughout the cabin. Rose and Fanny began our tour in the back of the airplane.

The airliner began to move. Ginny clasped her hands. Herb looked intently out the window, his leather folio resting in his lap.

After a short taxi, a rush of power took us skyward in a speeding smooth leap and although visibly tense, Ginny seemed to relax almost as soon as we were airborne.

"How'd you like that?" I asked her.

"Not bad. In fact, it was kind of fun."

"Next time you might want to try a window seat," Herb said with his face set square to the glass looking out at the falling earth. "It's a whole new perspective looking down from up here. Things become very small."

"No thanks," replied Ginny. "I don't think I'm ready for that."

A few minutes passed. I began to read a magazine. Then, with a child's curiosity, Herb reached up and pulled the telephone off the headrest in front of him. As he examined it, his smile refreshed. "These are new since the last time I flew."

"When was that?" I asked.

"1975." He put the phone back and reached for SkyMall catalogue. I haven't had a reason to fly until now. Don't remember these either," he held up the catalogue. "Imagine that, shopping for things at 30,000 feet."

"Maybe you can find something to buy," said Ginny.

"I doubt it," Herb replied. "I've lost most of my need for things." Herb looked to me, "Say, Randy, I need to tell you, tomorrow I will not be joining the group."

This was a surprise. "Really? Why not?"

"I will be out and about making deliveries." Almost imperceptibly, he grasped the folio in his lap. "I'm sure I will miss most of the day."

"What are you delivering?" I asked.

"Copies of my book. Would you like to see one?" Before I could answer, he had his folio up and open. From inside he removed two paperback booklets, over a hundred pages thick, glossy white cover, black type, inauspicious to say the least. Bound, with a glued spine, the cover read, "The Book of Truths." He handed one to both Ginny and I, and said, "I had these made in a little print shop not far from where I live. They do nice work, don't you think?"

"Very nice," I said and opened the cover. "All things are possible," was all that was printed on the entire first page. I turned to the next page, "Risk should be measured by reward." Next page, "Listening is an acquired skill." I jumped to the middle, "Opportunity is where you find it." Again. "Balance should be applied to most things."

I looked at Herb and smiled, "You're right, there's a lot of truth in here." When I tried to hand it back, he said, "Please keep it. Consider it a gift from me to you."

I thanked him and so did Ginny as she read and turned a page.

"So, who are you delivering copies of your book to?" I asked.

"Publishers," he said. "New York is full of publishers and I'm hoping one of them might see fit to publish the Book of Truths."

"Well, good luck with that. I hope you know, you are going to miss an excellent tour of the city."

"I'm sure the tour will be exceptional, but a man has got to do what a man has got to do."

I slipped Herb's book in my briefcase which was sitting on the floor under the forward seat. Ginny continued to read.

"We know this is Ginny's first flight," I said. "Herb, what year did you first take to the sky?"

"1949. I was 51 years old. My son and I flew in a DC-3 to Montana, for a fishing trip."

"Why, that can't be right," said Ginny putting down her book. "That would make you ninety-eight years old. "

Herb nodded an affirmative response.

"Really? Ninety-eight?" I asked.

He nodded again.

Both Ginny and I were a bit struck. "I would have guessed early eighties maybe, but never ninety-eight."

"Thank you, I guess. To tell you the truth, today I'm feeling about forty-five." He leaned closer and said in a tone full of mischief, "Today is the beginning of a new adventure, and I am as excited as a six-year-old on Christmas Eve."

"Ninety-eight years old," I thought in disbelief. In my mind I could not help but question Herb's honesty. "Where were you born, Herb?"

"I was born in a little three-room farm house outside of Dodge City, Kansas, January 27th, 1898. It's not there anymore."

"Who was president?"

"McKinley."

"Amazing."

"What?"

"You just don't appear to be nearly a hundred years old."

"There are days when I feel every bit of ninety-eight. But it really is true, you are as young as you feel."

"So what's your secret?" I asked.

"My secret?

"Your secret to long life?"

Herb widened his grin and raised a brow. "I have many, but I don't pass them along to just anyone."

"Why not?"

"There are some people who don't deserve to live long." His grin broke into a smile.

I paused and pondered his statement for a moment, wondering if his comment was directed at me, then asked, "What would it take to convince you I'm worthy?"

"Oh, I think you're worthy enough, Randy. I'm just not sure you're ready. I didn't figure them out until I was fifty or sixty years old."

He said the words with a conviction that took me by surprise. "You probably never had a drink in your life."

He replied, "There were times when alcohol was my only friend. These days I enjoy Kentucky bourbon over ice, but I bet it's been more than 30 years since I could say I was drunk."

"Did you smoke?"

"Cigarettes from 1917 to 1926, cigars off and on over the years. I tried marijuana for the first time around 1920."

Ginny's eyes widened and she looked up from the book. I couldn't help but let a little puff of surprise exit my lips.

He continued, "We called it reefer back then."

"Nothing wrong with your memory," I said.

"Sometimes I have to concentrate to remember details, but for the most part, I remember everything from around 1904 or '05. I even remember my telephone number from 1939."

"You were raised on a farm?" Ginny asked.

"My father grew anything he thought we could sell. Mostly wheat, hay, corn, and beans. Farming is a hard living. I was glad to get away from it. How about you?" he asked Ginny.

"I was a small town girl. My father worked selling building materials in a lumber year."

"How old did your parents live to be?" I asked looking for a genetic link to Herb's longevity.

"My mother died six days after giving birth to me. It was February 1st, 1898. She was 20 years old. My father delivered me in their bedroom. The nearest help was miles away, and if you lived in the country, chances were good you would be born at home. I think it was a lack of cleanliness that killed my mother. My father probably didn't wash his hands. She became infected and with no drugs to fight it off, well Dad said she just kind of faded away. They called it childbed fever back then."

"How awful," said Ginny. "You know, it was not that long ago, giving birth was the most dangerous thing a woman did."

"How about your father?" I asked. "How old did he live to be?"

"Dad lived just long enough to see his farm ruined by the Dust Bowl. He was sixty-one when he died. Without a doubt, the hardest working man I have ever known." A reflective bit of silence passed before Herb continued. "I am the last of my line."

"You don't have any family?" Ginny asked.

"No blood relatives I know of. Outlived everyone – a stepbrother and sister, two wives, a daughter and a son. So far as I know, I don't even have a distant cousin alive."

"Ninety-eight… the things you must have seen." I said.

"You have no idea," he replied.

"What one thing sticks out as the most memorable event of your life?"

"Oh, I could never narrow it down to just one. I don't know if I could even narrow it down to a hundred. Could you?"

I thought for a moment, "Maybe man walking on the moon."

"Everybody says that, and I grant you it was a memorable event, but it has been an interesting century. Sometimes I cannot believe I was alive before Orville and Wilber Wright flew their first airplane. Now look at us, 30,000 feet in the air flying at 500 miles an hour. Can you imagine?"

"The Depression?"

"Lived most of it in despair."

"The Dust Bowl?"

"Happened right there where my father had his farm. I was living in Texas in the 30's raising a son. Dad lost both his farm and his life in 1934. The bank took his farm. Pneumonia took his life. Did I tell you, he was the hardest working man I ever knew? "

"Did you attend college?" I asked.

"Not a single day," Herb replied. "But I often wish I had. My formal education ended at the end of sixth grade and I have been trying to catch up ever since. Dad took me out of school to help on the farm. I always resented him for that because I liked school and did well when I was there."

15

"Did your father go to school?"

"Dad didn't learn to read until he was a teenager. He figured if I could read and write, that was all the education I would need. I also think he didn't want me to be smarter than he was."

"Did you ever consider going back?" asked Ginny.

"To school? No, not really. One thing led to another and back then it was not nearly as important as it is today."

"What year did you finish?"

"Let's see, I would have been about twelve so… that was 1910."

"One room country school?" I asked.

Herb lifted a brow. "Oh no, we were highfalutin'. We had two rooms, but only one coal stove, so in the wintertime, everyone was in the one heated room. I remember my first teacher was an angel. Miss Trego will always be my first love. She had a thick head of auburn hair she usually wore up in a bun, a thin face and a very small waist. She may have worn a corset. When outside, she kept her face shaded under a fancy parasol. I bet we had the best dressed and the best looking teacher in Kansas that year. I had a big crush on her, but then, so did all the boys. After less than one year, she married a man from a couple of towns away and left us to have a family of her own. I remember all of the children crying the day she told us she was leaving. Even the older kids were upset.

"Our next teacher was a bitter, mean, angry farm girl from our community named Ethel Brophy. 'Course nobody could replace Miss Trego, but Miss Brophy never tried. Fact be known, she was not even a teacher. Miss Brophy was judged by the local town elders to be the smartest person available to step in. She was a tall woman with huge breasts; had no teaching skills. What I remember most about her is that she liked to throw things. One day she picked up my slate and slammed it down my desk causing it to crack in half. 'See what you made me do,' she said. 'If you'd learn how to spell, things

16

like that wouldn't happen.' Course with her it was always someone else's fault."

"I bet you even remember the word," said Ginny.

"Oh I remember every detail. The word was longitude. I had left off the 'e'. That 'e' cost me five cents I was saving to spend on getting in to see the freak show at the county fair. It was a hard lesson to learn. I never did get to see that freak show."

"What was the lesson?"

"Life is not fair."

"How old were you?" I asked.

"Third grade. That night I told my father what happened and of course, he sided with Miss Brophy. I don't think he could have spelled longitude on his best day, but he made me spend the only nickel I had on a new slate."

Ginny said, "Sounds to me like Miss Brophy should have paid for it."

"I'm sure I would have agreed. If I am remembering right, the only reason they hired the woman was because she claimed to have read more than a hundred books. One day a real teacher became available and that spelled the end of Miss Brophy. Mrs. Holtz, her replacement, was very strict, but always fair and I never saw her throw anything. She wasn't much to look at, but that was probably better for learnin' purposes. It would have been good for me if I could have stayed through the eighth grade."

"World War I?" I asked knowing Herb would have been of age.

"Army Doughboy, France, 1917."

"You served in World War I?" Ginny asked.

"It was my ticket off the farm."

"I can't imagine what that must have been like," I said.

"And you should be thankful for that."

"Bad memories?"

"One bad spot on a twisting, turning road. I've found my way through more than a few bad spots. Everyone has them.

But I will tell you this, few things in my life compare to what I witnessed in Europe, 1917. Evil, sorrow and waste… I'm sure World War II was much the same. For that matter, I'm sure every war brings out the worst in people. It certainly did in me. I'm sure the next war will once again take young men and teach them the finer points of how to be extreme."

"Let's talk about happy memories," Ginny chimed. "We're on vacation. What are your happiest memories, Herb?"

"My first wife. The births of my children. Some of my favorite times were spent in the mountains of Colorado. There are few things to me as pleasant as the sweet air and the quiet you can find in Colorado's Rocky Mountains."

"I would have to agree with that," replied Ginny. "Did you hike the mountains?"

"Did I? Still do. Although I don't know you can call what I do now hiking. Twice a month, late spring to early fall, we have a group from Seventh Heaven, that's the name of the home where I live, we go walking in the foothills. They call it meandering. Our activities director is good about finding flat mountain terrain lower than 9,000 feet."

"Seventh Heaven looked like a very nice place," said Ginny. "I was impressed by what I saw when we picked you up. The property was beautiful."

"Yes, it's cosmetically nice. But I would not recommend it unless you are ready to cash in your chips. They watch us as if we are in day care. The food is not so good. I'm suspicious of their constant questions. How are you feeling Mr. Conroy? Did you have a bowel movement today Mr. Conroy? Excuse me but it's none of their business how often I use the toilet. Don't get me wrong, I'm not antisocial, but sometimes I long to be alone. I guess I miss the total independence I enjoyed just a few years ago."

"Why don't you move?"

"Where would I go? Fact is, there are some good people working there, and let's face it, at ninety-eight, I need a little help."

"Tell us about your wife," said Ginny.

"Wives, actually. I had two."

"Then start with the first one," I suggested.

"That's a long story from long ago."

"Longer than four hours?" I asked glancing at my watch.

Herb turned to Ginny and then back to me, then again to Ginny, took a slightly larger than normal breath and began. "Claire, my first wife, was working the morning shift at a little cafe where I stopped to get breakfast one summer morning in 1923. I was 25 years old, living in Kansas City, Missouri, and it seemed to me that I could do no wrong. Like most 25 year-olds, I was cocky. Hell, I thought I was immortal and had good reason to feel that way. I survived World War I. On two occasions, I wouldn't have bet a dollar on my chances of leaving Europe alive. Somehow, I managed to get through it with little more than scrapes and scratches, but I came home a different man.

"Anyway, home from the war, I was hired to be a salesman. I sold tools to hardware stores. I had a brand new company paid for Model T, an expense account, and all the gasoline I could burn. At that time, a lot of the money I made I spent on foolishness. Work kept me busy during the day. Speakeasies, bathtub gin and Kansas City jazz occupied my nights. Kansas City was quite the place back then. The "Paris of the Plains" is what they called it. Probably as corrupt a place as any city of the day. It was fun. Oh boy, you could visit clubs all over town and see bands like Joe Sanders Nighthawks or maybe the Bennie Moten Band."

"What year did you say it was?"

"1923."

"Prohibition?" I asked.

It was automatic the way Herb lifted his left brow. "You know your history, Mr. Perkins. Yes, Prohibition was in full swing, but that never stopped anyone I knew from taking a drink. Anyway," he continued, "back to Claire. I stumbled into the diner where she was working one morning. Hungover, I'm sure I looked a mess. Claire was a skinny little brunette who came over to my booth to take my order."

"Was it love at first sight?" Ginny asked.

"Not at all. At least not from my side of the room. I can't say I even noticed Claire that day. She was an attractive person in a plain, uncomplicated way. I grew to love the sight of her. But she was not physically beautiful and she was not the kind of woman I was interested in pursuing. I was looking for a flapper. A girl who could party with me all night long. I thought my type of woman was flashy and stylish, always ready for a good time. Claire was anything but. She had just the hint of an overbite, thin lips, straight brown hair and matching brown eyes with a nose as round as a marble at the tip. She was five feet tall, skinny, but deceptively strong. Anyway, that day, all I was interested in was breakfast. I ordered French toast with a side of peanut butter, scrambled eggs, toast, bacon, and a glass of orange juice. Having oranges year-round was kind of a new thing back then. The next thing I know, Claire brings over a big glass filled to the brim with juice. There must have been three large oranges squeezed into that glass. It was so thick with pulp you could float a spoon on it. If you ever had a glass of fresh squeezed orange juice, you know what I mean. I can taste it now, pure liquid sunshine. It was better than good. It was sweet, energizing, nectar of the Gods. To this day, I cannot look at a glass of orange juice without thinking about Claire and that little Kansas City diner where we met.

"Well, the next day I didn't go back because I was interested in Claire, I went back for another glass of orange juice. And she brought me one. She brought me one every morning for a month. And then one day, sitting at the counter because there wasn't a booth, I ordered my usual and just as usual, Claire brought over a big glass of juice. As I'm eating, a man sits down next to me. Claire steps up to take his order and the guy points at my food and says, 'That looks good, honey. I'll take the same.' Well, a couple of minutes later she comes over with a tiny glass of juice. That glass couldn't have been more than three swallows. 'Say babe,' he says to Claire, 'what do I have to do to get a big glass of juice like that?' Claire stepped up close to us and said to the man so only he and I could hear, 'Mister, I'm not your honey, I'm not your babe, and I don't serve juice like that to just anyone.' Then she looked at me with an expression that was nothing less than perturbed. It was as if she was saying with her eyes, come on, when are you going to ask me out? That was the first time I really took notice of Claire. It was my first indication she had her eyes on me or that there was anything special about my glass of juice. I looked around the diner and sure enough, anyone who had juice was drinking it from a tiny little three-swallow glass. Later, after we had been married for a couple of years, she claimed from the moment she saw me, I never really had a chance. Claire picking me was one of the best things to ever happen in my life. 'Course, I didn't realize it while it was happening, but now I know every day with Claire was a precious gift. If I could have one wish, it would be to have any one of those days back with Claire. She possessed a powerful mix of insight and passion. If she became passionate about you or your cause, you might as well give in. I've been lucky and had a lot of happiness in my life, but those years I had with Claire were extra special. She was my first true love. I thought I had loved before Claire, but the fact is, I mistook lust for love. It's a common mistake among the young. Claire's love was as warm and comforting as a heavy blanket on a cold wintry night. I've been loved since then, but no one was ever able to give me that same feeling of assurance Claire somehow did. I know now, that talent is a rare and wonderful thing."

"Wow, what a tribute," I said.

Ginny agreed.

"There are many things I might not ever have learned had it not been for Claire. She intuitively knew more about me than I may have known about myself. And it wasn't just me, Claire could look at a person and somehow know what they needed. She could be as tough as a lumberjack or as loving as a lap dog, and all the while, she shaped the world around her with a kindness that was truly rare. I don't mean to make her seem like a saint. Like everyone, she had faults. She talked in her sleep and when she was nervous, she bit her nails. That used to drive me nuts. Sometimes she was bullheaded and seldom took no for an answer, but in all my years, I never knew anyone with a warmer heart than Claire."

A flight attendant arrived with the beverage cart - a cup of coffee for Ginny and I, a glass of orange juice for Herb. " See," he said holding it up, "They just don't mak'em like they used to," he chuckled. The skin around his eyes wrinkled and from the expressions on his face, you could almost see the memories coming to light inside his head.

"In 1924, my employer transferred us to Denver. We bought a house and got a dog … I remember one night I arrived home tired and testy from the struggles of my day. Claire was putting together our dinner when I walked to the kitchen, stopped in the doorway and secretly watched her work. Her back was to me. She was standing over the sink, wearing an old housedress and apron. I had seen her in that dress at least fifty times, but for some reason, that day she seemed to radiate in the tired old thing. Our Victrola was playing "IT HAD TO BE YOU," and Claire was humming along."

"We had a Victrola," said Ginny.

"Claire didn't have much of a voice, but that never stopped her from singing. Especially if she thought she was alone. She slightly rocked to the music, singing and peeling or washing something over the sink. At that moment, I remember feeling all of the problems of my day disappear. I remember wondering what did I do to deserve this wonderful woman. Her slight sway, the off-key hum, the way she tucked her hair behind her ear to keep it out of the way. I startled her when she turned and found me standing in the doorway. Clutching her breast from the surprise, she picked up a wooden spoon and lovingly hurled it at me."

Herb lifted his glass and took a sip of juice, then continued. "The cutest thing about Claire was her smile. Have you ever noticed, all people are pleasant looking when they smile. It's hard to be unpleasant and smile. Anyway, Claire had a way of curling her lip when she smiled. The only way to describe it is to say, it was sexy. She could curl her lip into that devilish little smirk and it always mesmerized me. When she smiled like that, she could get me to do anything.

"That night, after dodging the spoon, I stepped over to her, wrapped my arm around her waist and just ever so slightly, pulled her close. We stood there for the longest time laughing, kissing, holding each other not wanting to ever let go. It was a good fit when we held each other. We ended up eating dinner late that night, some of it cold, some of it burned.

"Once we were on our way to a baseball game," Herb continued almost without pause. "We were late and I was anxious to get to the park, so I took a shortcut though a neighborhood. Suddenly Claire said, 'Stop, stop the car.' I did and she jumped out and ran back down the street. I thought maybe she had seen something on the road, but in my rearview mirror, I watched her turn and trot into someone's yard. I backed the car and pulled over only to find her picking up laundry that had blown from a clothesline. 'Claire,' I yelled, 'don't bother with that. We're late.' She just kept right on picking up clothes, folding them neatly and placing them on a chair on the porch. Within a couple of minutes she was finished and back in the car. 'You don't even know those people,' I scolded. 'What difference does that make?' she argued back. 'If it were your best shirts blowing around the yard, wouldn't you appreciate someone taking the time to pick them up? Maybe they had an emergency and had to leave in a hurry.

Maybe they are at the hospital right now with a sick child. Maybe they were summoned to someone's deathbed.' Then I tersely said, 'Maybe they are napping when they should be taking in the laundry. Or maybe they are at the ballpark sitting in seats that would have been ours.' Claire just shook her head and smiled at me with her loving grin. Discussion over, I drove on.

"Did Claire work?" Ginny asked.

"Clair worked very hard at everything she ever did, but while she was married to me, she never worked a job for money. How old are you, Randy?"

"Thirty-eight."

"Did your mother work outside the home?"

"Some, but not when I was young."

"Ginny, did you have a job?"

"I was a homemaker."

"Claire was very good at making our house into a home, but it bored her tremendously. She liked to be in motion, near the center of whatever was going on. I used to get angry with her because she didn't know how to relax. What I did not realize at the time was, being busy was how she relaxed. She'd move from one thing to another and didn't stop until she had accomplished her task. Things that would have seemed like chores to most people filled her with joy. Our garden was the best on the block. You couldn't find a weed in our yard. I mowed and fertilized and did anything else she needed help with or wanted done, but the vision was hers and it was nothing less than beautiful. Claire volunteered everywhere, church, schools, the Red Cross, fundraisers, food drives... she always made time. She liked to bake and we were often carting around cookies or cakes or something she had whipped up. Our house always smelled of baked goods. The aroma was heaven's scent."

"Oh yes, I remember that smell." Ginny turned to me and said, "Everyone baked back then."

"But what Claire really excelled at was being a mother, and on the 10th of May 1926, she gave me the greatest gift of my life when she gave birth to our daughter, Lisa. My God what a day that was. You can imagine, with my mother dying after my birth, I was as nervous as a dog up a tree. But things had changed a lot since I was born. Lisa was born in a hospital. I made sure we had the best doctor in town. If I could help it, I was going to do everything I could to make sure nothing was going to go wrong. I waited in the waiting room most of the entire day. Back then they sent the men off to wait in a room. It was terrible. I would have much rather been with Claire. After what seemed like hours, the doctor came out, shook my hand and congratulated me on the birth of my daughter. He said everything was excellent, both mother and baby were as healthy as could be. Then they took me to the nursery and showed me my little girl. I have to tell you, my first sight of her left me a little shaken. She was wrapped in a white blanket and all I could see was a wrinkled little face with the oddest point to her head. I mean she had a sharply pointed head. I asked the nurse about it and she told me not to worry, lots of babies look like that, but I was skeptical. I mean, it was really pointed. I thought my God, that can't be normal. I looked at some of the other babies in the nursery and none of them had strange looking heads. Don't misunderstand me; I fell instantly in love with my little girl. She was pure joy, but the shape of her head had me concerned. I had grown up on a farm and seen many animals give birth, but I could not remember a head that looked misshaped like Lisa's did. To tell you the truth, I worried she might be retarded. When they finally let me in to see Claire, she lay exhausted in bed, half awake, half asleep. I asked if she had seen Lisa and she nodded. I asked how did she look and Claire replied, "her head is a little pointed but the doctor says she'll be all right."

"I don't suppose you have pictures of Claire and Lisa?" Ginny asked.

As a matter of fact," Herb shifted his weight left, withdrew his wallet, and from inside removed a photo pressed in a protective plastic sleeve. The slightly faded, battered and tattered black and white print displayed an image of a woman with a little girl upright in her lap. Their resemblance left no doubt this was a mother and daughter. The girl held a doll under her arm. A cocker spaniel sat with them to the side.

"As you can see," Herb said, "Lisa's head rounded out nicely. She was all girl, as girly as a girl could be. See how she's holding her little doll? Claire and Lisa were quite the pair. I have a special memory of them combing each other's hair. This picture was taken about a month before they died."

Ginny looked up at Herb. "You lost both of them at the same time?"

Herb nodded. "They were in a traffic accident. It was a cold gray day, January 20th, 1930. One morning they left the house to do some shopping and never came home again. It was a Monday." Herb ran his finger over the top of the plastic sleeve as if to clear it of dust or finger prints. "Denver had electric streetcars at that time. You could catch it at the end of our block. Claire and Lisa had taken one downtown. Actually, they were downtown shopping for a birthday present for me. The streets were icy that day and on their way home, a truck slid out of control and collided with the streetcar they were riding. The thing was full of people, but they were the only two who didn't survive. Lisa was killed instantly. Claire was hospitalized with very serious injuries. Everyone else involved walked away from the accident with bumps and scratches, and to this day, I believe it was Lisa's death that actually caused Claire to die.

Ginny uttered, "Oh my gosh."

"Two days after the accident, Claire briefly regained consciousness. She opened her eyes, and in a low whisper asked where she was. I told her there was an accident, that she was in the hospital. She asked about Lisa and when she saw the sorrow on my face, she knew our little girl had died. She never said another word, just slowly closed her eyes. Two hours later,

26

she was also gone. If Lisa had survived, I'm sure Claire would have found a way to recover. Instead, I believe she chose to be with our little girl."

Ginny lifted her hand to wipe away a tear.

"There were many days after that day when I wished I were also dead. A couple of months passed before I put everything we had in a friend's garage, sold our house, quit my job, bought a used Model T Ford and started driving. I must have cried a million tears on those old two-lane highways and dirt roads. For the longest time, I blamed myself for their deaths. After all, if not for my birthday, things could have been very different."

A quiet settled between us. Three people in somber thought.

Truth #54
Search for good in everyone,
but realize, sometimes it isn't there

It was Ginny who brought us back to a common place. "Where did you drive?" she asked Herb.

"Nowhere in particular. In the first year, I found myself walking the beaches of both coasts three or four different times. Long distance pacing is what it was. I drove by many things, but I can't say I saw much of anything. I crossed the paths of many people, but I can't say I stopped to talk to anyone. Everything I saw reminded me of what I lost. The sight of a little girl would start me to sobbing. There were many things that affected me that way. I would hear a song on the radio or see a woman that reminded me of Claire and I would find myself overwhelmed with remorse. I avoided places where mothers might be with their children. Something as simple as a glass of orange juice might push me over an emotional edge. I became a flesh and blood ghost wondering aimlessly among the living. I avoided being noticed so nobody noticed me. Months piled up, one on top of the other. Two years were gone in the blink of an eye. I spent all of that time wondering, why me? Why them? Why? I thought a lot about killing myself, but knew that was never really an option. I wondered if I would ever stop feeling pain. Now I know it does get better, but with a wound as deep as that, the pain never goes away. I learned to live with it. 1930 and 1931 were empty years – without a doubt, the most difficult time of my life."

"Where did you end up?" I asked.

In October, 1932, my Model T broke down in Dallas, Texas. It was going to cost more to fix it than it was worth so I ended up selling it for scrap. Have either of you ever been to Texas?"

I nodded. Ginny shook her head.

"Some of the friendliest people you will ever meet live in Texas. They've got some real scoundrels too, but I liked it there. Anyway, in 1932, I still had not come to terms with what had happened to Claire and Lisa. I wasn't broke, but I was existing like I was and I'm sure I looked like some kind of hobo. Which is what I was. I had lived out of my car for more than two years. Then, after being in Dallas for a week or two, I was walking down Market Street one morning on my way to the building that housed the Work-for-Food program."

"Work-for Food?" I interrupted.

"Yeah. You showed up in the morning and they would send you out to do odd jobs. You might unload trucks or sweep a street or any number of things. Then they would feed you a sack lunch at noon and a hot dinner at the end of the day. This was before FDR's New Deal. Anyway, on this particular morning I was stopped by a man standing outside. His name was Roger Crockett. He was big guy, 6'4", 240 pounds, 47 or 48 years old, a complex man who could be as pleasant as a spring day or turbulent as a tornado. He had eyes I often thought could see into my soul. He said he had a need for men with strong backs who didn't mind working long days for good pay in the oil fields. He promised three dollars a day to start, plus a cot in a tent.

"Three dollars a day?"

"Listen, that was big money. The depression was raging in most parts of the country. Good jobs were hard to find and Crockett promised if I stayed on for a month, he'd raise my pay to five dollars a day. It didn't take long for me to accept the offer. Myself and five other men went with him to an oil field a hundred miles east of Dallas and I'm here to tell you, that job was just about as dangerous as the trenches of France during World War I. The pay was better and you didn't have to sleep with one eye open, but if you didn't pay attention, you could lose your life or a limb at any time.

"The men who worked those oil fields were as callous a collection of leather-tough souls as you could ever want to meet. But once they knew they could trust you to do your job, they adopted you as one of the boys. It reminded me of the army in some ways, except I carried a big wrench instead of a gun. We lived in a collection of tents that resembled our bivouac in France, but better. The oil camp had everything you might need – a general store, an eatery, a saloon. Everything could be taken down and moved in less than a day."

"Sounds like quite a life," said Ginny.

"Brutal is what it was. But I had nothing better to do and the routine of it all helped me forget. Work and sleep was all I did. It was probably the best thing that could have happened to me at the time."

"Was Crockett related to Davy Crockett?"

Herb scoffed, "He wanted you to think so, but I found out later it wasn't even his real name. In Texas, the name Crockett is right up there with Jesus and George Washington. His real name was Felix Schickerman. Changing his name was a business decision." Herb sat up, arched his back and continued, "Crockett was many things and when he saw an opportunity, he was quick to act. By the time I arrived in the oil camp, he had built himself quite a little racket. Officially, he worked for and ran the drilling crews for Plains Oil, but the truth was, he set things up for himself. He even had his own police, if you could call'em that. These were men you didn't want to mess with; a couple of brutish thugs who would just as soon spit in your eye as give you the time of day. As a sideline, Crockett collected a percentage from anyone who tried to sell anything or do any kind of business in his oil camps. There was a man who ran a little mobile general store, a couple of woman who did our laundry, every time you had a meal, if you got a hair cut or if a carpetbagger rolled in selling wares, Crockett collected a fee. What the man had done was set up his own little mini economy. He paid us in company funds and then as it circulated in camp, he took a piece at every stop. Sometimes a big piece. By the time the money had circulated a couple of times, most of it found its way into his pocket. He was a master of making sure you didn't need to leave camp to spend your money, and to do that, he brought in prostitutes and gamblers. He even charged for showers."

"How much?" I asked.

"10 cents. And some of the men refused to pay it, or would drink away all their money, or lose it gambling and then not be able to afford to clean up. I've smelled many unpleasant things in my life, but something I remember most about those days is the smell of being around some of those men. They could gag you with their B.O. There was one guy you could smell long before you saw him. Someone would say, 'Here comes Ed,' and sure enough, Ed would show up. This guy was so filthy, no one would let him sleep in their tent. He had a roll of blankets and seemed content to sleep under one of the company trucks. I haven't thought about stinky Ed for thirty years."

"How long did you work the oil fields?" I asked.

"Mmm, let me think – I was there for a year before I got remarried and another four years after that. I guess at least five and maybe six years."

"Tell us about your second wife." said Ginny.

Herb hesitated and then swallowed as if to keep bile from welling up from his stomach. He turned to Ginny and said, "My second wife was nothing like Claire. In fact, Ramona was very much the opposite. I try to make it a rule not to speak ill of the dead, but that's a chore whenever Ramona comes to mind. 'Bout the only good thing I can say about her is, she gave me a son."

"How did you end up with her?" I asked.

Ginny jumped in, "Maybe Herb would rather not talk about it."

I looked to Herb and he said, "It's not a pretty story, but I don't mind. After roughneckin' for about eight months, Crockett came to the rig one day and pulled me aside. He said he wanted to introduce me to his daughter Ramona. He said he thought we should meet. Now this was really something because everybody knew Crockett kept a tight leash on his daughter and she was not to be courted. But he said if I was so inclined, I could take her to a movie. Well, I was not so inclined. My head was still clouded by the fog that came the day of Claire and Lisa's accident. Besides, Ramona was 14 years younger. I was not ready to be involved with anyone, let alone the boss's twenty-year-old daughter. I didn't know it at the time but Crockett had been watching me. For that matter, he watched everyone - knew all the gossip - knew whenever anyone came or left the camp. It was like those canvas tents had ears and eyes. Crockett noticed that except for essentials – food – showers – clothes, I hadn't been spending any of my money. Most of the men would spend every dime they had on whores or gambling or booze. Some of them would send their money home to families. My dollars just piled up in a deposit box I held at a bank in Gilmer, Texas. I didn't trust savings accounts back then, so the box became full of cash and somehow, Crockett knew this.

"One Friday, he showed up again at the rig where I was stationed and this time he invites me to dinner at his house. This was highly unusual. The men in my crew didn't know what to think. Nobody could remember anyone ever being invited to Crockett's house, let alone a roughneck who was low man on his crew. Well, I was always one to figure, when the boss asked you to do something, you had better do it. I didn't want to, but what could I do? Crockett was not the kind of man you said no to. He told me to leave the rig early and get myself cleaned up. Then about five o'clock he came around in his car to pick me up.

"Crockett and Ramona lived in a house in Gilmer. At dinner that night, he made small talk while I sat across from Ramona and nervously ate my food. She and I didn't say more than a dozen words to each other. Crockett did all the talking. Then about halfway through the meal the telephone rang. It was a business call and before it was over, Crockett had become a little heated. After he hung up, he cursed a streak of blue, looked at us and said he needed to go to Dallas. At first, I thought he meant in the morning, but he left the table, packed a bag and as he was leaving said he wouldn't be back before Sunday morning.

"Did Crockett have a wife?" asked Ginny.

Herb nodded, "But by that time, she was long gone. The story from Ramona was she died of a brain hemorrhage, but I heard talk years later about how it was Crockett who used a bat to hemorrhage her brain."

"He murdered her?"

"According to that account. Another rumor was, she fell in love with another woman and the two of them ran away."

"Another woman?" I asked.

Herb shrugged a shoulder and nodded.

"But you ended up married to Ramona?" Ginny asked.

Herb nodded. "Ramona seduced me into her bed that very night. After dinner, she invited me to sit out on her porch. Crockett took the car and I didn't have any way to get back to camp. She kissed me and it awakened something that had been dormant for years. She was a willing temptation and I was not man enough to resist. I remember closing my eyes and imagining she was Claire. When I left the next morning, I left Ramona pregnant."

"Oh my," said Ginny.

Herb again removed his wallet and pulled two photographs from inside. "This was my son, Harry." In the first photograph, a ten-year-old boy stood with a huge, grin on his face. His hand sat on top of the head of a Springer Spaniel. The dog's tongue was curiously sticking out from his lips. In the second photograph, the boy was now a man, dressed in a uniform, he appeared to be in his early thirties.

"Very handsome," said Ginny. "Was he a policeman?"

"Fireman. That picture was taken at a ceremony where he was awarded a medal for bravery; he rescued two of his fellow firemen from a collapsing building."

"You married Ramona because she was pregnant?"

Herb nodded. "If she had not been, I never would have married her. After she was, I didn't give it a second thought. I wasn't going to let any child of mine be considered illegitimate. If she was going to be the mother of my child, then she was going to be married to me. But two people could not have been more different. It didn't take long for me to discover she was an angry person. We fought a lot. Looking back now, I suppose she had a right to be. She was dealt a bad hand. For her, nothing was ever right and that showed itself in a wicked and angry soul. She was cute when I first met her, but after Harry was born, she let herself go. She had a cigarette in her mouth from morning until night. I'd come home, open the door and cigarette smoke would roll out of the house. I'd complain about it and she'd blow smoke in my face. Harry was sick the first two years of his life. I'm sure it was from all that smoke. I came home to the sound of Harry crying almost every evening. His diapers would be soiled or he'd be hungry. His crying would stop as soon as he saw me because he knew I was there to take care of him. Ramona was a terrible mother. The worst I have ever known."

"She didn't love your son?"

"Ramona didn't know the first thing about love. You know, love is not innate behavior. A parent's obligation is to show their children how to love. That was a lesson Ramona never had. Anyway, not long after Harry was born we fell into a routine where I went to work, Ramona stayed with Harry, then I'd get home and she would hand me our son and go next door to be with her father. Harry and I wouldn't see her until the next morning."

"Next door?" asked Ginny.

"Crockett put up a house right next to his and that's where Ramona and I lived. Nothing fancy, but a whole lot nicer than the tent."

"Why did you stay married?" I asked.

"Divorce Ramona? I thought about it damn near every day those first three years, but I worried she would take Harry and I was not going to let that happen under any circumstance. Harry was everything to me. It was Harry who rescued me from despair.

"Then one day when Harry was five, the four of us were having a meal – Crockett, Ramona, Harry and me. After Harry finished, he went out to the yard to play and Ramona started clearing the table. As she passed her father, she bent down and whispered something in his ear. Crockett sat up in his chair and said, 'How would you feel if I asked you to take Harry and move to Dallas?' Crockett was never one for beating around the bush. He said, 'There's a school in Dallas I think would be good for Harry. I can get you a job at company headquarters and help you get set up in a house. I'll pay Harry's tuition. He deserves a better education than the schools can give him here. Do you think that might be something you would be interested in doing for your son?' I have to tell you, I could not have been happier had I won the lottery. In only a matter of weeks, Harry and I were living Dallas. I had a job dispatching trucks for the oil company. Harry started school. Crockett even hired a woman to be our housekeeper."

"What happened to Ramona?"

"Oh that was the best part, Ramona stayed with her father. He was the only person who could ever really keep her under control. She fought me like a tiger with a flaming tail, but I never once heard her so much as raise her voice to her father."

"She abandon her son?"

"Like he was nothing more than a bad memory. Ramona was the worst mother I ever knew. Crockett showed up regularly in Dallas; at least six or seven times a year. Whenever he was in town for meetings, he'd have dinner with us. He'd bring gifts to Harry, and tell him his mother missed him. He said, 'Your mother would be here but she has a sickness in her head.' 'Course Harry was smart enough to know his mother didn't care about him. After a few years, Crockett quit mentioning her all together and we didn't ask. Our lives were better without Ramona. In Dallas, I worked Monday through Friday. In the oil field, I sometimes worked seven days a week. I coached Harry's baseball team for a couple of years. Harry played saxophone in the school band. We learned to play chess together. We talked about almost anything and everything. The best thing I ever did and the most fun I ever had was the time I spent with my son."

"Did your housekeeper live with you?" Ginny asked.

"No, Gabriella gave us three days a week. The rest of the time, she had a family of her own to take care of, a husband and four boys. She did our laundry, shopping and became a very good friend to both Harry and I. She was really the closest thing to a mother Harry ever had. Our families were close. Her husband and the boys were always welcome at our house and we spent many occasions with them at their home. Together, our families listened to the news of World War II on our radio. The President's address after the attack on Pearl Harbor; the announcement of the atomic bomb dropped on Japan… those were serious times, but I must say, those years brought back a happiness and comfort to me I had not known since Claire and Lisa.

"Then, just about the same time I began to feel tragedy had lost sight of me, our world came apart when Ramona found her way back into our lives. There had not been a peep from her in seven or eight years. Then, one sunny afternoon, Gabriela called me at work and said I should come home right away, that there was a woman who wanted to see me. She said she was crying and distraught. When I walked into my house I found Gabriella sitting in the living room with a rather round, sobbing woman who had a very pained expression on her face. I bet thirty seconds passed before I realized it was Ramona. I never would have recognized her had I passed her on the street. The slight, little person who had seduced me into her bed in 1932 was now 250 pounds of sorrowful being. Because Crockett had told me she was crazy, I didn't know what to expect. She said, 'Daddy died from a heart attack. He dropped over dead after laughing at something Jack Benny said on the radio.' I told her I was sorry and asked what I could do? That's when she reminded me we were still married. She said, 'I want to come live with you. You have to take me. I don't have anywhere else to go.'"

"Oh my God," said Ginny. "I mean, I'm sorry. What did you do?"

"Well, I told her that wasn't going to happen. I knew Crockett must have left her a pile of money, so I wasn't worried about what she would do. But I should have been worried. You see, Ramona didn't know the first thing about how to function in the outside world and her heart pumped hate and anger through her veins. She functioned within Crockett's little universe and she was only calm when he was there to tell her what to do. With Crockett gone, Ramona didn't know the first thing about how to behave.

"I think I know a little bit of how she must have felt," said Ginny in a low mumble. "That's a terrible place to be."

I nodded as if to tell Herb to continue.

"When Harry arrived home from school that day he was as shocked by the sight of his mother as me. She stood up from her chair and said, 'my goodness, you are the image of your father,' She hugged him and began to blither more tears. Harry stiffened like a block of stone and gave me a look I had never seen from him before; confusion seasoned with revulsion and an urgent need to break away."

"How old was Harry?" Ginny asked.

"Fifteen. At dinner that night, Ramona again asked me if she could come and live us. Harry exploded at the suggestion, 'No,' he barked. 'Why would we want you here? You never cared about us. We haven't heard from you in years. I didn't even remember what you looked like.' I tried to calm him down. 'Dad, if you let her live with us, I'll run away. Look at her...' I told him she was not going to live with us. Then Ramona, with a hate that emanated from the core of her soul, said to both of us in a low, growling voice, 'Herb is not your father, Harry. Your father was my father and our father is dead.' Harry and I looked at each other with a moment of confused, disjointed contemplation. Then like a lightning bolt passing between my ears, I realized what she was saying. 'Oh God,' Ramona said in a near whisper, 'what have I done? I promised daddy I would never tell anyone.' 'What does that mean?' Harry asked. All Ramona could do was again mumble, 'My God, what have I done?' Harry ran to his bedroom. I followed close behind and closed the door. He asked me if I knew what she was talking about. I reminded him Crockett said she was crazy. Then Harry asked me about how we all came to be. As I told him the story, everything fell into place and he could see it on my face as I realized Crockett was Harry's father and I had been duped into thinking he belonged to me."

Truth # 96
You do not have to share the same DNA to be family

Ginny and I sat speechless.

Herb continued, "Crockett and Ramona knew she was pregnant when he invited me to dinner that night. Crockett watched me enough to know that I would be easy to manipulate. In all of my life, I have never met anyone who could manipulate the way he could. It's a sad fact that people who possess that skill cannot refrain from the temptation to abuse it. Crockett recognized I was somehow damaged and he used me to conceal the fact that he had impregnated his daughter. I also think he suspected I would be a good father to his son."

Herb's eyes showed the weight of his words but at the same time, his face still held his ever-present grin. There was no sadness in his demeanor. He seemed to wear the experience as a badge of honor. Without prompting, he continued. "I know it's an awful story, but I don't hold anything against either of them. In many ways I am forever grateful. That night I told Harry in no uncertain terms, I was his father. He was the best part of me and no matter what, he would always be my son. He said, 'I know, Dad. I'm just glad you were there to rescue me.' And that is the best compliment I ever received from anyone.

"Ramona was gone when we came out of the room. Two days later, I was at work when someone from the oil camp called. The voice asked if I was Ramona's husband and it pained me to acknowledge I was. The voice said, 'I'm sorry to tell you this over the telephone, but your wife is dead.' This is terrible to admit, but the news brought me a sense of relief. Ramona found her way back home and once there, she went into the bedroom and hung herself from the ceiling above Crockett's bed. I had not thought she would take her own life, but in hindsight, I should have considered it a possibility."

Ginny put her tray in the up position, unlatched her seatbelt and began to get up. "Excuse me, gentlemen." I stood up and let her into the aisle. "I'll be right back." She made her way to the rear of the airplane.

"I hope I haven't offended her," Herb said.

"Oh I don't think so," I replied. "So what happened after that?"

"Well, Harry and I inherited everything Crockett and Ramona had. It was a substantial amount for the day."

"What year?"

"1948. It took five months to wrap up Crockett's affairs. After it was over, I asked Harry what he wanted to do and after weighing the options, we both agreed it was time to leave Texas. We could have gone anywhere. Harry didn't care where. We needed the distractions of different surroundings. We needed a place to make a new life and forget. But before I could begin to do that, I knew I had some unfinished business back in Denver. You see, I had never begun to deal with Claire and Lisa's death, and I somehow came to the conclusion I had to go back and see what was left of my life with them. I was determined to close all the open chapters of my life before beginning another.

"Before I left Denver back in 1930, I stored most of our possessions in some unused space at a friend's garage. We were in contact every so often, probably two or three times a year. Then in 1935, the Merkle's contacted me to ask if their daughter and her new husband could use some of our old furniture to set up house. I gave it all to them as a wedding present; the furniture, Claire's cookware, the plates and silverware... It seemed good to me that newlyweds would be setting up a home with our stuff. Claire would have wanted it that way. The only things I asked them not to take were the items I had boxed up -- our clothes, Lisa's toys, Claire's knickknacks, our pictures, all of our personal items. For eighteen years, those boxes collected dust in the corner of Ernie Merkle's garage in Denver, Colorado.

"I sold our house in Dallas and Harry and I gave away most of the rest of everything we had. We decided not to bring anything that could not be packed up and hauled in the back of a brand new 1948, fire engine red, Nash pickup truck. It was Harry, our dog, and me. Harry was just learning to drive. You should have seen how excited he was the day we bought the Nash. He picked it out and drove it more than I did. In fact, three or four years later I signed it over to him. You're too young to remember Nash trucks, aren't you?"

"I've heard of Nash, but I can't say I know what they looked like."

"In its day, it was top of the line. They quit makin'em in 1954. When were you born?"

"1959."

"From 1946 to 1954, Nash only made a few thousand trucks. I wish we had kept ours. Harry took care of it and had he not sold it, it would be worth some dollars today. We broke that truck in on the roads between Dallas and Denver. Our new Nash didn't like the thin air of Colorado until Harry figured out the carburetor needed an adjustment. After that, it ran like the wind and purred like a kitten. Harry always had a way with machines."

"So you moved to Denver?"

Herb nodded, "At first we rented a house in south Denver. Harry went to South High School and was quick to make friends. Once we decided to stay, I bought a house in the same neighborhood. I've called Denver home ever since."

"So what kind of work did you do?

"Actually, our move to Denver brought with it my retirement. I had not intended to retire. It just worked out that way. I was 50 years old and had worked most my life, had always been able to save money and with what we inherited from Crockett, I figured why not take a year or two off. At the time I was hoping to live to be sixty-five. Can you imagine? Harry and I settled into our new life. He went to school. I did some volunteer work at the V.A. and took a couple of part-time jobs just for something to do. But I was lucky. After Dallas, I never had to work another full-time job. I managed our money and played the stock market a bit. Harry was first to get a job. That spring in 1949, the two of us went to an amusement park. We had a great time riding the rides that day. There was a roller coaster, a fun house, and arcade. There were sideshows, beautifully landscaped gardens, a summer theater, and the

Trocadero Ball Room. Anyway, as we were getting ready to leave, Harry asked if we could come back tomorrow. Right about the same time I noticed a sign on the gate that read, *Help Wanted.* I nudged Harry and jokingly suggested, 'Maybe you should get a job here then you could come every day.' Just like that a seed was planted. Harry asked, 'Really? Would you let me?' I told him, 'Might as well. It's about time you learned how to make some money. You're already pretty good at spending.' We went to the office where Harry filled out an application. They hired him to start the next day. What he wanted to do was be a ride operator but you had to be sixteen to run the rides. Harry was a few months short of that, so they gave him a choice of cutting grass or being a sweeper, someone who walks around the park sweeping litter and emptying trash.

"You know, it was that job that inspired Harry to be a fireman. One afternoon I was listening to the radio when a news flash interrupted the program. They announced there was a fire at the amusement park, three stations were responding and there were injuries. I dashed for the Nash and sped over there, but when I arrived, they would not let me in. You can imagine how worried I was. From a distance, I could see it was the Fun House on fire. I looked at all the faces of the people milling about but Harry was not among them. After a few minutes, I decided I could not stand around and wait, so I circled the park and found a spot where I could climb over the fence. Once inside, I moved toward the Fun House all the while looking frantically for Harry. By that time the fire was all but out and the building was a smoldering heap of ash. I asked some of the other employees about Harry but no one had seen him since before the fire. I was nearly starting to panic when all of a sudden I heard Harry call out, "DAD!" I looked around but could not find him. I heard again, "DAD, I'M UP HERE!" I looked up, there was my son, standing on the roof of the Trocadero Ballroom, his face covered in soot and sweat. He and another boy had buckets in their hands and smiles on their faces so big you would have thought they just saved the world.

I've got to tell you, finding him safe was the biggest relief I ever had. Turns out Harry and his friend climbed up to the roof of the ballroom just so they could watch what was going on. Smoke and burning cinders began blowing their direction and they soon found themselves stomping out a flurry of flaming ash. The chief of the fire department said if they had not been up there, the historic Trocadero would have gone up in flames for sure. When the owner of the park heard what the boys had done, he gave them both lifetime passes. And from that point on, Harry knew he was going to be a fireman. Not anything, not anybody was going to change his mind about that."

"With free passes," I asked, "did Harry continue to work at the park?"

"Not for long. You know, Harry always had money. He inherited half of Crockett's estate."

I could see Herb's mind was racing with memories. He spent some time reminiscing in his head before he said, "It was a good decision to move back to Denver. At first, I was worried the place would make me crazy with grief, but that never happened."

"So you found the closure you were looking for."

"Yes, I did. After retrieving my boxes from Ernie Merkle's garage, I put them in the basement of our rented house. A month or so later, while Harry was working at the amusement park, I mustered the nerve, went downstairs and started opening boxes sealed years earlier with string and tears. The first box was small and full of little trinkets, knickknacks and things. There were souvenirs from trips we took to Yellowstone and California. There was campaign literature, buttons and ribbons from the 1921 presidential election. Claire and I volunteered for Harding. Did you know that was the first election to allow women to vote for president?"

"Man, you are really old."

Herb raised his brow at the comment and let his smile conform into a grin. "Anyway, every item in every box held a memory. I smiled and cried a lot that day. It was an incredible experience. You know, after eighteen years, some of their clothes still held the faint scents of my wife and little girl. In one of the boxes I uncovered Claire's journals. I had known Claire kept a journal but I had never tried to read it. I would catch her writing from time to time, and she would always close the book before I could glimpse a word or two. She didn't hide it from me but asked me very early in our marriage not to read it. Everyone needs privacy and some space to pursue their thoughts. One of the things most precious in our marriage was trust. There were times when I would find one of her journals on our nightstand or sitting on her chair in our room. Sometimes a new book would replace the old and I knew Claire had filled another volume. But I never opened any of them because she asked me not to. I knew if I did, it would betray a trust. Even if she never found out, I would know. Actually, I struggled with opening those journals that day in 1949. But I did, and as I read, it revealed our life together from Claire's perspective. I discovered things about myself I had never known.

"In all, there were seven volumes covering her life and thoughts from a year before we met until the day before she died. There were poems about love and summer and our daughter and the dog. There were dates containing a single sentence describing everything happening that day. There were passages five or six pages long filled with observations about something that had her attention. It could be a recipe or an idea for one of her projects. In those pages, I also discovered the things Claire had seen in me. What we are is so different when you look from the inside out. You only know who you are when you can see yourself as others do, from the outside looking in.

"At times Claire saw me as her hero. At times, I was nothing less than a goat. Many of her observations caught me off guard. There were things I read in those pages she never let on during our marriage, opinions kept silent. She said she loved the way I looked at Lisa, and the way we felt in intimate moments, and how most of the time we were two who had somehow become one. She said it was not our commonalities that brought us together, it was our differences and how those differences somehow compensated for each of our shortfalls and strengths."

"Sounds like you had a wonderful marriage."

"We were good together, but it was not all peaches and cream. Claire hated the way I sometimes talked down to her and pointed out I could be arrogant and rude. She said the way I ate spaghetti was nothing less than obscene and she could not understand why I left my dirty clothes laying around the room. She wished I could be more tolerant and she said sometimes my fuse was short when confronted by little, insignificant annoyances. Since reading that, I have always tried to be more tolerant and to keep my anger in check, to pick up my clothes, to eat spaghetti without making a spectacle of myself, and to never talk down to anyone. Those have all been big challenges. Sometimes they still get the better of me.

"I remember one passage in her journal when she was upset because I refused to take dancing lessons. Dancing was big in the 20's. Everyone our age was dancing Foxtrots, the Charleston, the Footloose Strut… but I wouldn't dance. She wrote in her journal she was sure I would be a good dancer, that I had rhythm and had a musical heart."

"Didn't you say you liked jazz?"

"We both loved music. But I didn't feel comfortable dancing. Maybe it was because I thought we would have time for dancing later in our lives. I can tell you one thing for sure. The next time a woman I was interested in asked me to dance, I was Johnny-on-the-Spot. One of my biggest regrets is I did not dance with Claire."

"You dance now?"

"Not anymore. I started dancing to big band music in the 50's and 60's. Almost every Saturday night at the Trocadero Ballroom - the building Harry saved that day in the amusement park. I highly recommend dancing."

"Is dancing one of your secrets to longevity?" I asked.

"No, but I'm sure it can't hurt."

Ginny returned from the back of the airplane. As I got up to let her in, Herb rose, dropped his folio on his seat and said, "While you are up, I think I should make a similar journey." He side stepped out into the aisle and moved toward the front of the airplane.

Settled back in her seat, Ginny remarked, "He's quite an interesting man, don't you think?"

"He certainly is," I replied.

"Do you believe he's ninety-eight?"

"Why wouldn't I?"

"He doesn't look ninety-eight."

"How old do you think he looks?"

"Maybe eighty."

"I would have guessed eighty-five. But what reason would he have to lie?"

"Well, of course you're right. I do not think Herb is lying to us." From her seat Ginny leaned toward the window to look out. "I guess I'm jealous," she said. "He's the freshest looking ninety-eight year old I've ever seen."

I agreed.

Truth #40
Some people are owned by their possessions

I passed a few minutes leafing through the pages of the SkyMall catalogue before a light tap touched my shoulder and I looked up to find Herb returned.

"Would you like the window seat?" he asked.

"No," I replied, "I prefer the aisle."

"Ginny?" he asked. "Would you like to try the window seat. There's a lot to look at out there."

"You don't mind?

"Not at all."

"Okay." With no hesitation, Ginny took hold of Herb's folio, handed it to me, and then slid over to the window seat. "I'll just sit here for a little while."

"This is quite the briefcase," I said standing so Herb could move easier into the middle seat. "I don't think I've ever seen anything quite like it."

"I would be very surprised if you were ever to see another like this one." Taking it from me he returned it to his lap. "It was hand made by a man in Denver, a long time ago." He ran his hand over the top and gave it a light caress.

"How long ago?" I had to ask.

"1930."

"66 years."

"Actually," he said again running his hand across the top, "this was the present Claire and Lisa bought for me the day of their accident."

I glanced to Ginny. She looked as I felt -- both of us struck by this news.

"They didn't have it with them at the time because they asked the maker to engrave it with my initials." He pointed at the leather flap above the brass clasp where the faint imprint H.C. was stamped into the hide. "It was delivered to the house the day after their funeral, the day before my 32nd birthday, 1930." Again, his hand slid over the top in a light caress.

I saw Ginny's hand glide to a gentle touch resting on Herb's forearm. He smiled and acknowledged her caring concern with a nod.

"As you can see," he continued, "over the years it has taken a beating as it followed me almost everywhere I have been. I didn't have it with me in Texas. It was one of the things I left in Ernie Merkle's garage. Since then, it has carried important documents and not so important letters and bills. Often it held only my address book, a note pad, maybe a sandwich and a newspaper. But you know, it has become such a part of me, I would carry it around empty if I had to. It's a physical link to

Claire and Lisa. I feel part of me is somehow missing when it is not around. Now it holds the Book of Truths."

I looked at the weathered leather folio and was compelled to touch it again, but resisted. Scratched and beaten, it had only gained character due to wear. At one of the corners the stitching had been replaced. Discolored, it's brown dye marbled into a myriad of colors, no two shades identical. A large flap with a brass clasp secured it closed. In design, it was a cross between a briefcase and a portfolio.

Herb continued, "I still wonder if they had bought me a tie or a shirt or anything else that day, things could have been so different. If only they had taken a different streetcar. I nearly drove myself mad pondering the possibilities. Since then my birthday's been bittersweet."

"How did you get past it?" asked Ginny.

"At some point, I'm not sure exactly when, I came to believe that nobody ever dies by accident. When the people around you step out of this world, all you can do is accept it and know it was their time."

Both Ginny and I were again at a loss for words. Every sentence Herb uttered seemed to deepen the pool of times and tragedies of his life. Yet, through every story, he maintained at least the hint of a smile.

As if to save Ginny and I from comment, the flight attendant arrived with sandwiches, chips and cookies.

"Thank you," said Ginny to the attendant. "I'm famished."

"Breakfast came for me about 4 A.M." I said. "Herb?"

"I had a snack in the terminal. I don't think I am ready to eat again." He slipped his lunch into a pocket in his portfolio. "We eat too much," he said. "Americans eat too much food."

"You're so right," said Ginny. "Not only that, we eat all the wrong things. I bet you eat your vegetables, don't you?"

"I eat a little bit of everything, but I don't eat a lot of anything. I do like raw vegetables. I find I am at my best when I'm just a little bit hungry. I'm sharper and in the moment. Hunger gives me an edge. I enjoy a filling dinner every now and then. A properly cooked steak is a work of art. But a full stomach makes me lazy and wanting a nap."

"You nibble throughout the day?" Ginny asked.

"I eat when I am hungry and then only enough to rid myself of hunger pains."

"Is that one of your secrets?" I asked.

Herb smiled and said. "Yes, I suppose it is. Another one is two teaspoons of honey every day."

"Why two?" I asked.

"Because one is not enough and three is too many. Did you know honey is the only food that never spoils?"

"No, I didn't know that."

"If you are ever in the wilderness and get a cut or scrap and start to bleed, put honey on the wound to keep it from getting infected."

"Were you a Boy Scout?"

"Harry was. I spent a lot of time outdoors. We considered Colorado's mountains part of our back yard. Hunting, fishing, backpacking and camping all over the place. In 1959, we were on our way home from a fishing weekend along the Arkansas River when Harry spotted a sign that read, *For Sale, 150 acres with stream.* A few days later, without saying a word to me, he went back to look at the property. A month later he owned it outright."

"How old was Harry?" asked Ginny

"Twenty-five."

"That was a smart thing to be doing at twenty-five."

"In hindsight, it was more than smart, it was visionary. But at the time, I thought he was out of his mind. He used a large piece of his inheritance. Paid for the place in cash. It's a good thing he didn't ask me. I would have done my best to try and talk him out of it. It was a nice section of land with a sweeping view of South Park. I never got tired of that view. But it was out in the middle of wilderness. It was land, a tiny stream, and a remarkable view. I thought, 'what are you going to do with this?' But it didn't take long for me to realize, to

Harry, it was worth every dime. I had seen Harry happy his whole life, but when he was at Elk Springs, that's what he named the place, it was happiness overflowing with peace-of-mind and pride.

"He immediately started camping there. I was welcome whenever I wanted to come along. It was nice because it was only a couple of hours drive from Denver. At the firehouse, Harry worked twenty-four hour shifts with forty-eight hours off. From spring until late fall, he often commuted back and forth from the mountains. For a present, the following summer in 1960, I hired a contractor to put in a small foundation. Then, over the course of a couple months, Harry and a few of his friends built the exterior of a three-room barn style cabin. I helped, but they did most of the work. After it was habitable, he took years to finish the inside. But by the time he was thirty years old, he had a paid-for house in the city and a cabin in the mountains sitting on a hundred and fifty acres of land."

"Did Harry ever marry?" asked Ginny.

"No," Herb replied. He paused for a moment and then blurted out, "Harry was gay."

"Oh," Ginny stammered. "I see."

"I didn't know until after he died. The fact is Harry kept this a secret from me throughout his entire life. You would never know it to look at him. I mean, he was a very masculine man. People were always trying to set him up with women. When he was in school, the girls would not leave him alone. His standard excuse for not marrying was work related. His job could be dangerous and he didn't want a wife and children worrying about him."

"Wow," I softly mumbled, "so how did you find out?"

"Harry's best friend was a man named Chris Pickford. They met when they were in their early twenties and remained close until Harry died. Chris camped and fished with us often. He was also married and had two lovely little girls. You would see Harry and Chris together and they were just a couple of guys. I often thought they acted like brothers. After Harry died, I found

49

letters Chris had written. I'm sure you can imagine my shock. I believed I knew everything about my son. But this was something he couldn't share. Now I'm thankful Harry had someone he cared for deeply. Learning about this the way I did, it tore my heart apart."

After a moment, Herb sat up in his chair and said, "Harry was as fine a man as anyone you could have ever known. He was a decorated firefighter who earned the trust and respect of everyone he ever worked with. Every day of his life I was proud of him. He was everything I could have hoped for in a son. But I am glad I did not know this about him while he was alive. Does that make me a hypocrite?"

I shrugged.

"The world was a different place forty years ago. By hiding that aspect of his life, Harry made sure it was never an issue. Had I known in 1960, I am not sure how I would have reacted. I'm sure I would have disapproved. I am also sure it would not have destroyed my love or respect for him. Nothing was going to change that. He was my son."

"Do you mind if I ask, how did Harry pass?" asked Ginny.

"Heart attack," Herb matter-of-factly replied. "He was forty-one years old."

"Oh my," Ginny exhaled.

"Didn't you say Crockett died of a heart attack?" I asked.

Herb nodded. "Crockett lived to be twenty years older than Harry, but they both died from massive heart attacks."

"Maybe Harry was genetically predisposed."

Herb let his head move in a shallow nodded. "I think maybe so."

"Did you stay in touch with Chris?" asked Ginny.

"Chris called me a few times to see how I was doing. Then I made the mistake of thanking him for being a special friend to Harry. I told him how I knew they were more than just close. After that, Chris never called me again. When I called him, our conversations were short and awkward. I wish I had never said anything."

"What happened to Harry's cabin?"

"It was mine until I sold it eight years ago. As Harry's next of kin, I ended up with everything he owned; a house in Denver, Elk Springs, his bank account, which had grown to a very tidy sum. Harry was good with machines and money. He had a knack for handling both. Last but not least, I also inherited his three year old golden retriever, Fred."

"Fred?'

"Lots of us grieved for Harry, but I don't think any living thing missed him more than Fred. Harry and Fred were inseparable. Those last three years, you never said here comes Harry. You always said here comes Harry and Fred. Fred went to work with Harry at the firehouse. He didn't go on emergencies, but if they were out and about doing inspections, or at a school giving a safety talk, Fred usually followed along. It was Fred who was with Harry when he died. They were at the cabin. Harry was moving a load of firewood from the back of his pickup truck when his heart beat for the last time. The doctor who did the autopsy said he was dead before he hit the ground. One minute you're here, the next minute you're gone. He looked very peaceful. You might have thought he was asleep."

"You found him?" I asked.

Herb nodded. "Someone from the firehouse called and said Harry didn't show up for his shift. They called both his house and the cabin before calling me. I knew immediately something was very wrong. Harry never stood-up anyone. He might be late or have to cancel, but he never left the people around him hanging. To put it in a word, he was reliable.

"Two of his coworkers picked me up and we went looking first at his house and then to the cabin. I had keys to both. The house was empty. No sign of Harry or Fred. All along the way, we scanned the road looking for skid marks or something that might indicate an accident. That was the longest drive of my life. Every mile increased my dread. Mid-afternoon, we turned off the highway onto the road that led to the cabin. Before we reached the house, Fred came charging down the road. He was unusually anxious and overly exited to see us.

"We found Harry lying on the ground between his truck and a stack of firewood. The three of us, actually I guess it was four if you count Fred, we stood there for the longest time. I think Fred was hoping we could do something. When we didn't, he lay down next to Harry's body and did not move until the coroner arrived. Fred was as sad as any of us that day."

Silence. A long, extended silence passed before Herb said, "I'm sorry. You both must think my life has been nothing but heartache and tragedy. I'll stop talking before I ruin your day."

'Please don't," said Ginny. "I'd like to listen to anything you have to say."

"You're a dog lover, aren't you?" I said in an effort to move the conversation.

"Absolutely. It seems to me through the majority of my life there has always been a dog around. I like cats too. I guess I like animals. But dogs hold a special place in my heart. A good dog will show you the meaning of unconditional love. When I was a kid on the farm, we had a collie named Sheriff. Dad called him Sheriff because his job was to keep the chickens out of the barn. He was good at it too."

"You didn't want chickens in the barn?" I asked.

Herb looked at me with a raised brow and said, " 'Course not. Chickens belong in the chicken coop. Everywhere they go, they make a mess. Dad trained Sheriff to keep the chickens out of the barn. We had cats in the barn, which Sheriff knew to leave alone because they took care of the rats and mice, but if a chicken found its way in, and they often did, it was Sheriff's job to make sure they weren't there for very long."

"Did he hurt them?" Ginny asked.

"Occasionally. Not often. Once in a while we would find him with a dead chicken, but he always had a very guilty and regretful look on his face. I think it was his way of dealing with a chicken who had come into the barn too many times. Usually he would catch 'em with his mouth, carry 'em outside and let 'em go. He'd sneak up on 'em or lay low between the stalls and wait. Then when a chicken would come around, he would chase 'em back outside. He was good at policing the barn.

Herb smiled. "One of my earliest memories is from five years old. On Sunday's we went to church and then to my grandparents farm for dinner. My grandmother had a medium sized poodle - a snippy bundle of white curly fur. His name was Buddy. My whole day involved avoiding Buddy. At that age, he was nearly as big as me, didn't like children, and if he had you cornered, he'd dart in and give you a nip on your ankle or elbow just to show who was in charge."

"That sounds awful," said Ginny. "You were five?"

Herb nodded.

"It's a wonder you learned to like dogs at all."

"Buddy was never much of a buddy to me. Then another dog I remember was a mutt who hung around the oil camp. This dog had a passion for chasing rocks."

"Rocks?" I asked.

"Yes. Stones, small rocks. You could pick up a stone and throw it into a pile of stones and that dog would go find the exact same stone in the pile and bring it back."

"Really?" asked Ginny "Why stones?"

"I'm not sure. I do remember he didn't give the time of day to a stick or a ball, but throw a stone and he'd fetch that stone all day long. Sometimes he'd show up and drop a slobbery stone in your lap."

"What was the dog's name?"

"Rocky," Herb chuckled. "He was a stray that hung around our tent because we fed him and would throw him a rock. You could take a rock and throw it into a pond or lake and Rocky would swim out and dive until he had found that same stone."

"How could he do that?" asked Ginny,

I said, "He must have been able to see it in the water."

"No, he'd smell it."

" I don't believe it," said Ginny. "In the water?"

"Yes. Rocky would dive, then pop up, blow a burst of water out his nose, and then dive again - over and over until he found the stone. Not just any stone, but the exact same stone."

'Wow, that's incredible."

"Whoever it was, taught Rocky to do that, didn't do him any favors. Most of his teeth were broken. I don't think Rocky lived very long. When I married Ramona, he stayed with the men in the tent. I lost track of him after that. Did you have dogs, Randy?" Herb asked.

"We had a family mutt when I was growing up. She was a good one. Smart, faithful and loving. We had to put her to sleep just short of her eighteenth year."

"Eighteen is old for a dog." Herb commented. "Claire had a little cocker spaniel named Molly. Molly followed her around the house. When Lisa was born, Molly became a little jealous, but she got over it and was a good dog. I left her with the Merkles when I put my things in their garage. Then, Harry and I had that Springer Spaniel you saw in the picture. His name was Joey. Joey loved to fish and chase a ball."

"He fished?"

"We had a little boat I put on the lakes and ponds around Dallas. When we came to Colorado, Joey had to learn to fish from the banks of the rivers and streams."

"What do you mean, fish?"

"Have you ever seen how a dog will get excited when you asked if it wants to go for a walk?"

I nodded.

"If you asked Joey if he wanted to go fishing, he'd give the same kind of response - jumpin' and hoppin' around like a puppy too excited to sit still - excitement stimulating every muscle in his body. In fact, his body would shake for minutes when we put him in the car. You could not talk about fishing when Joey was around."

"But how did he fish?" Ginny asked.

"He didn't really fish. What he did was watch us fish and then get in the way after we had something hooked. He would sit on the bow if we were in a boat.   I could never cure him of trying to help land a fish. He'd sit and watch our fishing poles. If they moved, he'd bark and run and hop around. If we were wading in the river, he'd try his best to be right there. I lost some big fish because Joey got in the way. After awhile, it became part of the challenge to land the fish before Joey could screw things up. Sometimes he'd grab'em in his mouth and take it to shore. Joey was never happier than when he had a fish in his mouth. The look on his face was the same sort of expression a cat has when it has caught a mouse. Joey loved to fish."

"Sounds like you do, too." I said.

"Do you fish?"

"Golf and fishing -- they're addictions," I said.

Herb looked to Ginny and she shook her head no.

"What kind of fisherman are you, Randy? Bait, spinners, flies?"

"I've done all of those, but fly fishing is most enjoyable."

"Aaaah yes. Standing in the river, the power of the water as it pushes past your legs, flipping a fly to exactly the right spot."

I finished his sentence for him, "And feeling a fish take your fly in its mouth and run with it up stream."

"Now that is excitement," replied Herb.

"Oh, you men," said Ginny. "You never really stop being boys."

"Thinking about Joey, he was the only animal I ever knew I think intentionally tried to make people laugh."

"Seriously?"

"Yes,"Herb nodded.

"How so?"

"Joey would get in the let's play position. Do you know what I'm talking about? Front paws and head down, butt up in the air with a wagging tail? Joey would hunker down then stick his tongue out from under his lips. If you laughed, he would often jump up, turn a circle, then hunker down and do it again. Maybe I'm just imagining that Joey made us laugh on purpose.

Maybe it was just that laughter seemed to follow Joey. He was always a happy dog. It was easy to be happy when Joey was around."

Ginny asked, "How long did you have him?"

"Joey lived to be twelve. Arthritis and cataracts got the better of him. Harry and I cried like babies the day we took him to the vet and put him down."

"Ever had a bad dog?"

"No, I guess I've been lucky. I can't say I have. I've known people with bad dogs. But I have a theory about that - ever notice how pets seem to take on the personalities of their owners?"

We nodded.

"I believe pets are reflections of their owners. Show me a bad dog and chances are good you will find an owner who is just as bad. I once befriended a woman with an out-of-control schnauzer. That creature was an obnoxious little menace, never housebroken, a yapping little terror who seemed to live for causing tension and distress. It didn't take long for me to discover the woman was much the same as her dog, an obnoxious mess. Only difference I could see was, she was housebroken."

"Do you have a pet?" I asked Ginny.

"I have a cockatiel named Pickles."

"Ah, birds, amazing creatures," replied Herb.

"You've had birds?"

"Never as pets, but I did become familiar with a pair of wild ravens."

"Ravens creep me out," I said. "I'm not sure why, but I have always connected them with death."

"Well, it doesn't help their image that ravens are quick to show up whenever anything has died. In medieval times, soldiers observed ravens following them into battle. They saw it as a bad omen, but in fact, the birds were just smart enough to know there would be lots of meat to eat after a war."

"That's sick," said Ginny.

"Is it? We eat birds. How do you think ravens feel about that?"

"Feel?" I asked.

"You don't think animals feel?"

"On a level that they are offended by our eating habits? No I don't think so."

"Well, on that we might disagree. Anyway, anyone who has spent time watching ravens will tell you what amazing creatures they can be. Unlike some of the people I've known, ravens are thinking creatures. They communicate, plan, and are capable of manipulating their environment. Ravens may be the most observant animals on earth. And while they are watching, they are not just admiring the scenery. There is a lot going on inside their heads. You know, they live thirty or more years and mate for life."

"Like ducks," said Ginny.

"Ducks may mate for life, but I also think they have a thing for threesomes. These two ravens were as committed to each other as any two creatures can be. I saw them protect each other and their offspring without thought of injury to themselves. I saw them quarrel like husband and wife. I always sensed they knew what the other was thinking. I can't prove it, but from what I saw, I believe they felt love for each other. For all I know, it may be a higher form of love than humans experience. Their dedication to each other was enlightening."

"The only ravens I know are Heckle and Jeckle," said Ginny, "the cartoon characters. Did you name your ravens?"

Harry and Fred were first to make their acquaintance. Because they were thieves, Harry named them Bonnie and Clyde."

"Oh my," Ginny chuckled, "what would they steal?"

"Food mostly, but also anything small and shiny. Coins, bottle caps, nails, screws... I once watched one of them fly away with a spoon from the picnic table. Find a raven's nest, and there's a good chance it will be decorated with shiny things.

In gold country, miners tell tales of finding gold nuggets in raven nests."

"Pickles is always surprising me," said Ginny. "I taught him to sing Beethoven's Fifth. Di di di dooo, di di di dooo."

"Some birds are highly intelligent creatures. Could be that all of them are brighter than we think. It might scare us if we really knew what was going on inside their heads."

"Do you think they are smarter than dogs?" I asked.

"Ravens, by any measure, are smarter than dogs. Our ravens were sharp, curious, cunning, self-aware, and full of structured thought."

"So give us an example," I said.

"I could give you a dozen examples. Let me see." Herb thought for a moment and then said, "I guess the best way to tell this story is to start from the beginning. When Harry's dog, Fred, was just a puppy, he put his food bowl outside at the base of a tree, a few feet from the cabin's deck. Within a day or two, the ravens discovered the bowl and pretty much claimed it for their own. Now at the time, Fred was small enough that he was dwarfed by the birds. Ravens can get to be pretty big and if puppy Fred got too close, all they had to do was nip at him with a beak, squawk or flap their wings and he would tuck his tail and run. It was somethin' to see the way they bullied him. Now I know if they had wanted to, they could have killed puppy Fred dead. But they didn't because they knew killing Fred would mean the end of their free meals and maybe even the end of them. Harry would have shot'em for sure if they hurt Fred. Anyway, all Fred could do was protest. As a puppy, Fred had a whining yap and a squealing howl that was laughable."

"Oh that's mean," said Ginny. "Why didn't Harry feed him inside?"

"I suppose Harry could have done a lot to stop it, but instead, he chose to egg them on. Often he encouraged the conflict. Especially if he had guests around. But I'm gettin' ahead of myself. That first year, Bonnie and Clyde had their way with Fred. I remember sitting with Harry on his deck having breakfast watching the ravens swoop in and chase Fred away from his bowl of kibble. Harry would say, 'Come on Fred, don't take that from those birds. You gunna let'em steal your food? You're supposed to be a bird dog. Come on Fred, go get them birds!' Puppy Fred would bark and pace, get frustrated then sit and howl as the ravens ate his chow. It was hilarious. When they had enough to eat, Bonnie and Clyde cawed a song of victory and flew away. Somewhat humiliated, Fred returned to the bowl and finished off what was left."

"That's interesting," I said, "but it hardly paints ravens as geniuses of the animal world. We used to have raccoons and foxes raid our dog's food."

"Hold on, Mr. Perkins. That's just the beginning. This story evolved over fifteen years. You can't expect me to tell it in a couple of sentences." He continued, "Winters at the cabin could be brutally cold. If a heavy snow fell, you might not be able to get in or out until spring. So, Harry would usually seal the place up in November and not return until March or maybe even April the next year. Well, by spring that year, Fred was thirty pounds heavier. He still had the spirit and lack of wisdom of a puppy, but now was a fifty-pound dog. Harry told me that spring, Fred guarded his bowl like it was filled with gold. Every morning the ravens would be waiting, but now Fred was big enough to stand his ground. If the ravens got anywhere near him, the hair would stand up on the back of his neck, he would dip his head and show his teeth with a menacing growl. He stood over that bowl and ate every morsel. For days, Bonnie and Clyde watched from the trees. Then one morning, Harry filled the bowl and noticed the birds were cawing a call he never heard before. He stepped up on the deck and saw a flash of black as one of the birds flew in and landed a couple of feet from the bowl. Fred lunged. The bird jumped and took to wing in a low and slow flight just out of Fred's reach. Fred, thinking he was close to catching the bird, pursued with enthusiasm down the hill. As soon as he was away from his dish, the other raven landed at the bowl, ate a few chunks of kibble and then snapped up a couple more and flew to a tree. Fred came prancing back, all proud of himself, and never knew he'd been robbed while away."

I asked, "You think the ravens planned that?"

"Absolutely. No doubt in my mind."

"That would be pretty amazing," said Ginny

"That's nothing. What was amazing was the way the ravens turned this little morning ritual into sport. Sometimes they didn't seem to care about the food. Sometimes they acted as if they were in it for the challenge and sometimes I thought they were having fun playing Fred for a fool."

"How could you know that?"

"They had a special limb in a tree near the cabin where they would rendezvous. Sometimes I'd see them meet up after a raid and pass the food back and forth between them. It was as if they were saying, 'you eat it, no, you eat it.' Back and forth they passed the food until one would drop it to the ground and the two of them would fly away, sometimes cawing an unmistakably happy song. It was as if they were saying, see you tomorrow, or maybe they were laughing at Fred. All I can tell you is it often felt to me as though they turned the event into a game."

"Did Fred ever catch 'em?"

"Yes. But only once. I'm not sure how it happened because I didn't actually see him catch the bird. Maybe the ravens were careless or maybe they got their signals crossed. I don't know for sure. That morning, I filled Fred's bowl and went back inside to get something to eat for myself. All of a sudden there was a God-awful screeching racket. I ran back outside and found Fred holding down one of the ravens with his paw. I yelled, "FRED!" and he looked up at me as if to say, 'hey, look I finally got one.' I swear he had grin on his face from ear to ear. But his celebration was short lived. That instant, the bird's mate flew in, landed on Fred's head, and with a sharp talon, it hooked and pulled out a half-inch chunk of skin. Well, Fred let go and ran to me with a yapping, pain-filled cry. The ravens flew to their rendezvous limb and started to caw like a couple of atheists who had suddenly found Jesus. I had never heard such a racket as that before. I think one may have been chewing the other out or maybe the one was asking the other if it was okay. They were still cawing when they flew away. I remember wondering if that might be the end of their raids, but the next morning they were back again. I don't know if the ravens were more careful to never let Fred get close, or if Fred decided not to ever get that close, but whatever the case, so far as I know, the animals never touched each other again."

"Which one did Fred catch?" I asked.

"I have no idea. Even when they stood right next to each other, I could never tell them apart. Harry claimed Clyde was slightly bigger than Bonnie, but I couldn't see it. To me they were mirror images of each other."

"And how long did this go on?"

"The game? Ten years. As Fred got older, he slowed down and the fracas was much less intense. But the game went on in one fashion or another right up until Fred died in 1984. The passion of the contest went from raucous to something resembling a halfhearted game of tag. In later years, Fred would sometimes let the ravens eat before he did. Bonnie and Clyde seemed to lose interest when the challenge of the game was gone. But they still showed up just about every day. You may think I am crazy for believing this, but the last few years I owned the place, I think they showed up just to check on me. Fred was gone and I was old and alone. It was probably my imagination, but they somehow seemed concerned."

"Did they ever get close enough for you to touch?"

"Oh no, they were never going to let me do that. They would let me approach to about ten or fifteen feet. Sometimes they would fly up to the deck or sit and watch me from a perch on the edge of the roof's gutter, but I never wanted them to get so familiar with humans that they simply trusted us. Many of us can't be trusted."

"Where did they nest?" asked Ginny.

"All over the place. So far as I know, they built a new nest every year. The first one I found was more than five miles from the cabin. They could fly back and forth in two or three minutes. 'Course, I was an old man even then, but it took me nearly two hours to walk within sight of that nest. I didn't find another nest for three or maybe four years. One year they built one about a mile from the cabin. Then it became too hard for me to be bushwhacking for miles in the wilderness. I never did find another of their nests, but then, I was too old to look."

"Did you live at Harry's cabin?"

"From early May through late October, I spent a lot of time up there, but it was never my residence. I would spend a week in the mountains, then go home to the city for four or five days, wash my clothes, shop, get the mail and pay my bills. Then it was back to the cabin. You have to remember it was only a couple of hours away and so it was nothing to go back and forth in the same day."

"The birds were on their own through winter?"

"Yes. I always left food for them, but it probably didn't last. The ravens weren't the only animals that liked Fred's food. Squirrels, chipmunks - there was a fox I would see pretty regular. One night I left a bag of dog food outside, and in the middle of the night, was shocked awake by the shrilling calls of a pack of coyotes as they tore that bag apart. That's a noise you don't forget. If there was a drought or the berries didn't come in the spring, then the black bears would raid my garbage. One year I remember, Harry shot a deer and put it out a mile or so distance from the cabin hoping the bears would go to it and otherwise stay away."

"Did it work?"

"He never told me about killing any bears, so it probably did."

"When did you quit going to your cabin?" asked Ginny.

"When I turned ninety, I decided it was too much for me to keep up with, too far to drive, too hard to get food in and out. So, I sold the place in 1988 to a dentist who tore down Harry's cabin and put up a ten room mansion he called his summer home. For me, that was a hard thing to do. Harry's ashes were spread up there. I buried Fred near the same spot. Some of my most pleasant memories are from that place. You could not beat it for ambiance and quiet peace."

Ginny again rested her hand on Herb's arm.

"I remember the day the movers came to haul everything away. It was summer and unusually hot for the mountains. Bonnie and Clyde sat off in the trees and watched everything going on. Items coming out of the house; strange people moving around... this was a lot of activity - maybe the most they had ever seen around the place. Then at some point in the afternoon, I think they realized what was happening. I honestly think they deduced they were never going to see me again. Maybe they sensed my sadness because it was one of the saddest days of my life. Whatever it was, they started a cascade of caws, kind of an alternating song where they would answer each other. Then they took to wing and did something I had never seen them do before; they circled overhead, over and over, all the while gaining altitude. It was like what you would expect to see from a hawk riding thermals higher and higher in the sky. I watched until they were mere specks, then I blinked and lost sight of them and they were gone. I looked around one last time at Harry's cabin, got into my car and drove away. That was eight years ago in July. I have never been back. I often wonder, what happened to Bonnie and Clyde."

Truth #47
Life goes fast
Ask anyone who is old

"This is your captain speaking," rang a voice throughout the cabin. "We managed to ride a bit of a tail wind today. Our arrival in Newark will be twenty minutes early. Those of you on the right side of the aircraft can enjoy a view of Manhattan as we approach for landing. To all of you, we appreciate your business. Thank you for flying our friendly skies. Flight attendants, please make ready for landing."

"That went fast," I said looking at my watch.

"Yes," replied Ginny as she visibly stiffened in her chair. "Is landing a scary process?"

"Not at all," I replied.

Herb said, "You know what pilots say, don't you? Any landing you can walk away from is a good one."

Touchdown involved only the slightest bit of a bump. Safely on the ground, we taxied to the gate and disembarked. Inside the terminal I gathered my group of travelers; everyone, including me, eager to begin our tour. A luxury van waited to deliver us to our hotel, an impressive black vehicle with a uniformed chauffeur. Within minutes, we were on our way.

We entered Manhattan via the George Washington Bridge. Along the way, I pointed out sights and gave a running commentary about the city's early history and some of the more memorable landmarks and buildings. By four o'clock, we were parked in front of the hotel where I asked everyone to please wait while I secured the keys to our rooms and checked us in.

"Mr. Perkins," greeted the clerk at the front desk. I didn't recognize him but he said, "It's good to have you and your group with us again. Everything is in order." He handed me a stack of envelopes containing room keys. "Let us know if there is anything you require. Oh, and one of your group received a package yesterday - Mr. Herbert Conroy. It's a rather heavy box. We will deliver it to his room."

Ten minutes later, I was back at the van. Everyone but Fanny Hosack patiently waited inside. Fanny was pacing the sidewalk. I called her over, opened the sliding door of the van and said to everyone, "Good news - they have not given our rooms away." A slight chuckle came from a few in the group. "We are spread out over much of the hotel," I explained. "In fact, I don't think any of us are on the same floor. Give the bellman a few minutes to deliver your luggage. Sometimes it takes them half an hour or so. If you need to reach me, my room number is 1535.

"Where do you recommend we eat tonight?" asked Rose.

"There are lots of options close by. In the packet of information I gave you this morning, you will find a map showing most of the restaurants and attractions in the immediate area. You will also find my business card in the packet. The telephone number is my cell phone. Feel free to call me if you need anything or have a question. As for food tonight, I can recommend the hotel's restaurant on the seventh floor. It has a great view overlooking Times Square. I am also partial to the diner on the corner. It is probably your least expensive option close by."

"Where is that?" asked one of the men.

I pointed, "You can see it straight ahead on the corner."

With a somewhat caustic tone, Fanny asked, "What are we doing tonight?"

"Tonight we have no scheduled activities. If you are tired from your day of travel, I would recommend you eat and then get some rest. This is an active trip and it is important you pace yourself. If you are looking for something to do, Times Square is just a short walk down Broadway. If you take Seventh Avenue ten blocks, you will run into Central Park. Would any of you be interested in riding the subway?" I asked. Half of the hands went up in the air. "Anyone interested should meet me in the lobby at seven o'clock and I will take you for a subway ride."

"How much does it cost?" asked one of the passengers.

"You can ride the subway anywhere you like for $1.25, but tonight if you come with me, it will be my treat."

"Isn't the subway dangerous," asked one of the women. "I've heard bad things about the subway."

The group seemed curious as to what I would say. "Some of you, maybe most of you, might have the impression New

York is a dangerous place. New York is like any other big city, and it certainly has its share of crime, but I think Hollywood and news reports from past decades have left people with the impression that this is a city full of murderers and thieves. The mayor has done a good job clearing out the riff raff. He's beefed up the police force to a point where you will see them just about everywhere. You will not find bums washing car windows for spare change at the stop lights. Times Square is a good example. In the sixties and seventies, you would not have wanted to walk Broadway unless you were looking for drugs, a prostitute, or some other form of trouble. For the most part, those days are gone. Or at least, most of those activities have moved to other parts of the city."

"Darn it," one of the men said in jest. His wife was quick to slap his shoulder and shoot him an irreverent stare.

"That said, you should still pay attention to everything going on around you. I don't want any of you riding the subway after midnight. Thieves are opportunists and if they see an opportunity, they will strike anywhere, not just New York City. Ladies, keep your purse tucked close to your body. If you can live without your purse, leave it at the hotel. Each of our rooms contains a safe inside the clothes closet. Instructions for using it are on the door. Please lock up any valuables you may have brought with you. We have never had a bit of trouble at this hotel, but there is no sense in risking a loss. Men, you might want to shift your wallet from your back pocket to your front. I'm not telling you this to scare you. I say this to all our travelers in every big city we visit."

"How long does it take to ride the subway and where are we going to go?" someone asked.

"We will be gone for about an hour and all we do is ride the train down the line for twenty minutes or so, then get off and catch another train coming back. If you've never ridden a subway, it's an interesting experience. How many of you think you want to go?" Eight of the twelve now indicated they would.

"Did you all remember to change your watches?" I asked. "We lost two hours flying here. Let's synchronize. My watch says it is now four-twenty-eight. If you want to come with me tonight, please meet me in the lobby at seven o'clock. Last but not least, let's talk about tomorrow. Tomorrow morning our city tour starts at 9:00 A.M. Please be fed and in the lobby ready to go about 8:50. Any questions?" Not a word came from anyone. "Okay then, welcome to Manhattan. I will see most of you in the lobby at seven o'clock."

Our chauffer helped everyone out of the vehicle. Herb and Ginny were last to exit the van. "Herb," I said. "Apparently a package arrived for you yesterday. A heavy box?"

"Perfect," he replied.

"It will be delivered to your room."

"I wonder," he asked, "could you tell me how far it is to 1745 Broadway?"

"1745," I repeated. "That would be about... four blocks up Broadway." I pointed.

"I am going to walk over this evening, just to be sure I know the way."

"What's at 1745 Broadway?"

"A whole building full of publishers."

"Would you like some company," asked Ginny. "I was going to ride the subway, but I'd be happy to go with you."

"No, no. You should take the opportunity to see the subway. I'm sure it will be far more interesting than tagging along with me."

An unmistakable expression of rejection displayed on Ginny's face. "All right then," she said. "Randy, I will see you in the lobby at seven o'clock."

"See you then," I replied. As the two of them made their way into the hotel, I headed down the street to get some dinner at the corner diner. I had just ordered a meal when my cell phone began to ring. "Randy Perkins," I answered.

"Randy, this is Fanny Hosack. Are you in the hotel?"

"Actually I am not, but what can I do for you Fanny?"

"Well this room is so tiny. I really think Rose and I are going to need more space."

I heard Rose in the background, "Fanny, there is nothing wrong with this room. Leave Randy alone."

"Mr. Perkins, this trip was not inexpensive. You flew us out here coach and stuck us in the back of the airplane. Now you have us sharing a room with hardly enough space to move around."

"I'm sorry Fanny, but all of our rooms are the same size. Generally speaking, hotel rooms in New York City are smaller than other areas of the country. You have to understand, the cost of everything in Manhattan is going to be higher than at home."

"Are you telling me there is nothing you can do about this?"

"We might be able to move you to a suite, but that will involve an additional charge."

"We've already paid and exorbitant price for this trip. Had I known it was going to be like this, I never would have come."

If only I could have been so lucky, I thought. "Fanny, would you like me to see about moving you to a suite?"

"How much extra would it be?" she asked.

"I'm estimating now, but probably anywhere from two to five hundred dollars…"

Fanny cut me off before I could finish. "Outrageous," she barked into the telephone so loudly I pulled the receiver from my ear. "You're telling me another room could cost five hundred dollars?"

"Per day." I finished my sentence. "This isn't Salina, Kansas, Fanny. This is Manhattan."

Silence filled the earpiece and then a click as she hung up her telephone. Having Fanny around was going to test my patience. I could feel it in my bones, and not only that, I thought I could almost smell her rancid breath over the telephone.

Music is a universal language everyone can understand

Six-fifty was upon me in no time. I did manage to do my paperwork and make a few phone calls after dinner, but all too soon, it was time to be heading toward the lobby. Upon emerging from the elevator, I was surprised to find most of my travelers grouped together waiting. Missing were Fanny Hosack and Herb Conroy. I looked at my watch and saw it read seven o'clock. A prompt group is always a good thing.

"Good to see you all," I said. "Are we ready for a ride on the subway?" Some answered while others just nodded their head. "Follow me," I said moving toward the front door.

The nearest station was a half block walk from our hotel, along the sidewalk, then down two flights of stairs and there you are. I purchased tokens and one by one, we moved through the turnstiles. "Okay everybody, the next train will be here any minute. I'm hoping we can all fit into one car, but just in case we get separated, here's our plan. We get on and ride for five stops, then get off, cross over to the other side of the station and catch the next train back here. Five stops. Everyone got that?"

"How long has the subway been here?" asked one of the women.

"Since 1904," I replied. "At least, that's when the first line opened of what we ride today. There was another subway that operated for a few years between 1870 and 1873. It was only 300 feet long and was pneumatic."

"What does that mean?" asked someone.

"It was pushed by air pressure created by giant fans. In reality, it was more of a tourist attraction than a transit system, but it was the first subway in Manhattan."

"Where was the very first subway?" someone else asked.

"Subways are a British invention," I replied. "The first subway opened in London in 1863."

"How do you know all this stuff," asked Ginny.

"That's my job," I replied.

The train arrived and I was relieved to be able to fit all of my group in one car. Rose McCracken made a point of sitting with me.

"Randy, I am sorry for the way Fanny has been acting."

"It's okay, Mrs. McCracken. No need to apologize."

"Please call me Rose. I must say, I'm embarrassed by her behavior. She had no reason to complain about our room. In fact, I think it's charming. We even have a view of Times Square."

"What didn't she like?" asked one of the women.

"She thinks it's a little small," replied Rose.

I looked to the rest of my travelers and asked, "Is everyone's room okay?"

"Wonderful... Great... Very nice..." came back unanimous responses.

We chatted in little clusters and people watched as the locals got on and off the train. Just before our fifth stop, I stood, "Okay everybody, this is where we get off."

The train slowed and came to a stop. As the door opened, I listened intently for a sound I was hoping to hear.

"Where's that music coming from?" Ginny asked as we all exited the train.

I knowingly smiled, "Let's walk over and see."

The soothing sound of a tenor saxophone sent ripples of music through the air. Standing at the same spot where I often found him was a short, pudgy, bald, black man named Clarence Jeffers. The notes he played flowed effortlessly from his instrument and were as pure and sweet as honey dripping from a spoon. Ten or so people stood watching. Our group doubled the size of his audience and when he saw me, he winked and moved into a medley of popular tunes. Clarence was good at judging an audience and was now tailoring his songs to music older folks would recognize. When he finished, a cascade of applause echoed in the subway station.

I moved toward Clarence, shook his extended hand and then turned to my group and said, "Ladies and gentlemen, allow me to introduce to you the world famous saxophonist, Mr. Clarence "the Stub" Jeffers."

Clarence gave a slight bow of his head and said, "Thank you. Randy. Thank you very much."

I continued, "You may not recognize Mr. Jeffers name, but I know you've heard his music a thousand times. What have you been up to Clarence?"

"Same old stuff," he replied. "Friday, I cut a track for a television commercial."

"For who?" I asked.

"Couldn't tell you, Randy. Some kind of detergent or some such thing. As long as the check don't bounce, I don't pay much attention any more." One of my ladies dropped a couple of dollars in his instrument case. "Thank you, ma'am. Thank you very much."

I continued, "Clarence has worked with just about every big name in music." I turned to him. "Care to drop a few names?" I knew what his answer would be.

"No, Randy. Those are just people. Most of 'em can't hold a candle to these good folks."

"Clarence is a little modest. You see, over the last thirty-five years he has recorded and toured with Frank Sinatra." A couple of my travelers gave an audible gasp, "Ray Charles, James Taylor and one of my favorites, Steely Dan."

"Did you really play with Frank Sinatra?" asked Ginny.

"Yes, ma'am, I sure did."

"Clarence has toured the world at least a dozen times. Isn't that right, Clarence?"

He nodded, "Yes Randy, I surly have.

"Now here he is to give you a private concert, in a subway station in midtown Manhattan."

"Did you arrange this?" asked one of the women.

"No, but I wish I could say I did. This is Clarence's spot. It's not unusual to find him here, but to see him is always hit or miss. He's a busy man."

"Why do you play in the subway?" asked another woman.

"Ma'am, this is where I come to practice. You see, I live in an apartment and my neighbors don't appreciate me blowing while they're trying to watch their television shows." Everyone chuckled. "So I come down here to practice and play for the people. Sometimes I make a little extra money at the same time."

Another of my travelers stepped up and dropped a five in his case.

"Thank you, sir." Clarence said. He put the mouthpiece between his lips and began a soft cascade of notes that evolved into an improvised medley of Sinatra tunes. About halfway through, Ginny stepped over to me and asked if I had a pen and piece of paper. I gave her my pen and a business card. When Clarence finished, she stepped up, asked for his autograph and he politely complied.

We listened for half an hour. Finally, I said, "Okay folks we better make our way back to the hotel." I turned to Clarence, dropped two twenties into his saxophone case and thanked him. Much of my job involves making memories for my travelers. Clarence had given us a great one to start the tour.

As we rode the train back to our starting point, everyone wanted to know more about Clarence. "How long have you known him?" someone asked.

"A couple of years," I replied. "I was waiting for a train when I heard him start to play a Steely Dan song I recognized. I walked over and listened. I'm a big Steely Dan fan. When he was finished I said, 'Man, you played that exactly like Clarence 'The Stub' Jeffers,' and he said, 'I should hope so seeing how that is who I am.' I thought, what is the world coming to when a world-class musician has to play for change in the subway? Later I learned what he told us today, he comes to the subway to practice so his neighbors don't complain."

"That was amazing," said one of the men.

"Yes," another agreed, "I'm glad we didn't miss that."

I added, "Clarence put four children through college with the money he culled from people waiting for the train."

Rose said, "I hope Fanny doesn't hear what she missed. It would give her one more reason to complain."

The train stopped at our station, and we moved as a group back to the hotel. Once inside the lobby, the woman who had been worried about the safety of the subway came close and said, "I just want you know, that was the one thing my family told me not to do on this trip."

"What? Ride the subway?"

"Yes. My son and daughter-in-law told me the subways are dangerous and to not go near any of them under any circumstances. I can't wait to get home to tell them what we did. In fact, I may call them tonight just to rub it in. Thank you, Randy. You will never know how much I enjoyed that."

She moved away leaving me feeling day one of our tour had concluded a success. Just as I was about to go to my room, the voice of Herb Conroy hailed from behind. "Mr. Perkins, did the group enjoy their ride on the subway?"

I turned and found Herb standing a few feet away. "Yes, I think they did. How was your evening? Did you find your way to 1745 Broadway?"

"Oh yes. You were right; it's an easy walk from here."

Herb's eyes held a look of excitement. He was having an adventure and was drinking it up. "I seem to remember you saying you like a bourbon every now and then. Would you allow me the honor of buying you a drink?"

Herb raised his brow, "Yes, a drink would be good, but I think you should know your money is no good in this bar."

We moved to the lounge and found a table in the middle of the room. The server was quick to spot us. "What can I get you gentlemen?" she asked.

I pointed to Herb.

"I would like a Kentucky Bourbon over ice," he said and pointed back to me.

"The same please." She left us and I said, "Herb, I really enjoyed listening to you talk today."

"Well, it's good to know I didn't bore you. Sometimes I get started and I don't know when to stop."

"Boredom was never a part of today's mix. From the time you folks arrived at the airport until just now, I don't think any of us have been bored. Tell me, was the ride this morning as frightening as everyone made it out to be? You did not seem as rattled as the rest of our group."

"I can tell you for sure it was an exciting ride. Your driver to say the least was reckless."

"Well, I'm sorry for that. Everyone seemed disturbed except for you."

"At ninety-eight, there's not much of anything that disturbs me anymore."

Our server arrived with drinks and said, "That will be $15.50 gentlemen. Would you like to charge this to a room?"

Before I could reach for my wallet, Herb handed her a twenty and said, "Thank you, I won't be needing any change."

We sat quiet for an awkward moment, then I asked, "So, what are you planning for your hundredth birthday?"

He grinned. "Since 1930, I let birthdays come and go without any need for celebration."

"You're not interested in a tandem skydive?"

"That would be tempting fate."

"You certainly have lived an interesting life."

"You think? I bet if you talked to just about anyone, they would have interesting lives to relate. If your life is not an interesting challenge, then what's the point? I guess I get extra points for longevity, but all in all, I'm sure your life has been equally as interesting. In fact, I bet your life is rich with experience. Look at what you do for a living. You travel the world and get paid for it. I bet you have stories you could tell all night."

"I suppose, but I must tell you, I was fascinated by the experiences you talked about today. Have you ever considered writing them down in a book?"

"Mmm, sounds like a lot of work, Randy. I'm retired, I don't work that hard anymore."

I mentally vowed to drop the subject, took a drink from my glass and broke my vow by saying, "You know what you could call it?"

"What?" he asked.

"You could call it Herb's First 100 Years."

His face stretched with a widening grin, "You know, I'm not crazy about your idea, but I love your title." He raised his glass in a toast. "Here's to my first 100 years."

Monday, December 9th, 1996

Truth #82
Only you can make your dreams come true

I did not worry, or even think much about Herb Conroy on Monday. There was no reason. Considering what he said, I expected I might not see him all day.

The rest of my group enjoyed a city tour of Manhattan, including lunch at and a tour of, Carnegie Hall. A local guide helped add facts and flavor to the experience - details and anecdotes only someone living in the city can provide. From Battery Park to Harlem, we weaved our way through Manhattan, spending time in the financial district, SoHo and Chinatown. We drove past the United Nations, the Met and Lincoln Center. Twice we had opportunities to walk in Central Park. For a six-hour tour, it included many of the city's essential sights, albeit if only for a glimpse while driving by.

We were back at the hotel by 3:30 in the afternoon. I then escorted six of the ladies to Fifth Avenue for shopping. Fanny Hosack bought a four thousand dollar bracelet for herself. The others appeared mostly concerned with finding Christmas presents for family and friends back home. Those who stayed at the hotel explored other diversions. Some napped, saving energy for the evenings activities. Others walked Broadway and Times Square.

Our activity for the night featured the Christmas Extravaganza at Radio City. By seven o'clock, I was stationed in the lobby, guiding everyone toward our driver and van. Mr. Conroy," I said to Herb, "Good to see you this evening. I didn't know if I should expect you. How was your day?"

"Very good, but I feel like I walked a hundred miles." His leather folio was tucked under his arm.

"Are you okay? You shouldn't overdo it."

"Yes, I'm fine, but my feet are sore. I should have brought a more comfortable pair of shoes."

Ginny saw Herb and came to his side. They chatted as they walked to the van.

In December, the whole of Rockefeller Center takes on a festive spirit making it a hub for holiday activities. Decorations adorn most everything; the skating rink draws perpetual crowds. A huge tree is always trimmed and lit to perfection. To top it all off, the Christmas Spectacular at Radio City is nothing less than a direct injection of spirit for the season.

As a venue, Radio City makes any show special, if only because of the unique character and history of the space. The theater's vast interior tends to make one feel very small when seated inside. Seating nearly six thousand, it is billed as the largest indoor theater in the world. The Christmas Spectacular perpetually stars the Rockettes, a troop of long-legged, high-stepping beauties that move with a remarkable precision and elegant grace. With a tingling combination of music, dance and special effects, Santa's entrance is always a magical happening. All through the show, the orchestra plays a score of holiday favorites. The entire production is a masterpiece of coordination. Sets change, the Rockettes dance, and Santa is all over the place. Not far from my seat, across the isle and one row ahead, I noticed a young girl maybe six or seven years old. Entranced by the excitement of all the activity, the look on her face was one of adoring fascination. She was utterly enthralled. With a glance down the aisle at my travelers, I found many of them displaying older but similar expressions of awe.

It was eleven o'clock before we were back to the hotel. All of us exhausted from the rush of a long, event filled day.

Tuesday, December 10th, 1996

Truth #21
To not try is a crime against one's self

I can sleep just about anywhere. I have been told I snore like a bear. I know it's true because sometimes I wake myself and find my throat dry as the desert and my sinuses numb from the roar.

After a restful, snore-filled sleep, Tuesday morning found me up and preparing for another busy day. A cup of coffee from the coffee maker in my room helped bring me alert. Out the window high above Times Square, I gazed below at a ribbon of taxicabs. Dotted with an occasional limo, truck, bus, or private car, the street emanated a constant rumble. The din rose and fell with changes in the makeup of traffic. Trash trucks growl with a mixture of electric motors, hydraulics and diesel, while cars emit a constant vibration that stays almost unnoticed in the background. The honking never really stops. It all falls together in an opus for the city. In some ways, the sound exemplifies Manhattan.

Across the street, in an office tower taller than our hotel, I watched people at work. A man sat busily laboring at a computer. In the window below, a woman moved in and out of an office gathering papers and organizing files. A few panes down, another woman chatted with a coworker using wild waves of her arms and hands to enforce her point. It would have been easy to sit and watch for an hour, but I did not have an hour to spare. I showered, shaved and made ready for a busy day. Coming out of the bathroom I found a folded piece of paper slid under the door. The note read:

"Mr. Perkins, Once again, I will not be joining you today, but I do plan to be with the group tonight for dinner. See you then. Herb Conroy."

Curious as to what he was doing, I picked up the telephone and rang his room. Six pulses passed with no answer. At the prompt to leave a message, I replaced the handset in its cradle without doing so.

My eleven passengers and I rode the ferry to Ellis Island. From the ferry, the view of the Statue of Liberty is unsurpassed. Of course, people can get off on Liberty Island if they want. My travelers usually prefer to spend the time exploring Ellis Island, learning about immigrants and how they entered the United States. Some of them had ancestors who passed through the island. If American history is of interest, it's an experience that should not be missed.

The day moved smooth at a pace befitting my travelers. Although you needed a coat, the December weather was comfortably mild. The view from the island was picture perfect - blue skies with light wispy clouds, no breeze, the skyline of Manhattan for a background.

"Isn't that beautiful," said Ginny Crawford as she came up to me as I admired the view. "You have shown us some great sights, but that," she said pointing at the Manhattan skyline, "is one I will never forget."

"Trip's not over. I might surprise you with one or two more."

"Herb was right when he said the city would seem familiar. Everywhere we go, I see things I recognize."

"It is a special city. It has something different from other cities. I can't put my finger on it. I guess every city has it's own feel and distinction as a place."

"Thank you for not leaving me at the airport."

"You're very welcome, but I think it was Herb who really convinced you to come along."

"Speaking of Herb, have you heard from him today?"

The tone of Ginny's inquiry again held more than a passing concern. Not a romantic interest, but that of companionship. If Herb was anything, he was easy to be around. "Yes, he left me a note this morning. It didn't say much, but he is planning to join us for dinner tonight."

Ginny smiled and lifted her camera to her eye. "What a picture." She clicked off a couple of shots."

"Why don't you let me take your picture with the city in the background," I suggested.

"Would you?" She handed me her camera and I backed up few steps, brought it to my eye and snapped her with the Twin Towers of the World Trade Center dominating the city skyline.

"Now, do you mind if I get a picture of you?" she asked as I handed back her camera.

"Sure," I leaned against the seawall and smiled.

"I'll send you a copy if this turns out."

We chatted some more and then walked to the dock as it was time to catch the ferry back to Manhattan. Two-thirty found us at the hotel with some unstructured free time. I offered suggestions -- Central Park, the museums, Empire State Building or Twin Towers. Some chose to rest before our night's activities. I ended up in my room where I utilized the time by pressing a shirt and making a few phone calls.

At five o'clock everyone gathered in the lobby - all of us including Herb. Ginny, obviously happy to see him, was at his side. But I could not help but notice a slight change in his appearance. To put it simply, he looked tired. The smile was ever-present, but not as prevalent as the day before. In his left hand, he carried his leather folio. "Good to see you," I said. "How are things going?"

He brightened up a bit. "Moving around this city can be exhausting."

"A good meal may help," said Ginny.

His smile widened and he said, "Yes, I'm sure it will."

Our driver delivered us six blocks to 30 Rockefeller Plaza for a dinner reservation at the Rainbow Room. A relic from the past, the Rainbow Room tends to transport its occupants back to the 1920's or '30's. A circular parquet dance floor slowly revolves in the center of the room as a twelve-piece band entertains. Tables draped in white linens line the perimeter. Tall windows look out on Manhattan from the 65th floor with the colorfully lit Empire State Building providing a focal point, standing sentinel over the bustling metropolis below.

"Oh my," I heard Ginny say as the Maitre d' seated our group. "I never expected anything as elegant as this."

"Yes," someone else replied. "This is an unexpected surprise."

"I would have preferred Windows on the World," Fanny Hosack remarked.

"You've eaten there?" someone asked.

"No, but I've heard it has the best view."

Our party of thirteen divided between two round tables. My table included Herb, Ginny, Fanny and Rose.

"Excuse me," said Fanny to Herb, "are you with our group? I don't remember you from yesterday or today."

Ginny jumped in. "Herb was with us last night at Radio City."

"Yes, but it is true, I've been absent during the day. I've been on something of a quest."

"I see. The rest of us are on vacation, but you are on a quest?"

"In a manner of speaking." Herb lifted his folio from its place on the floor, "Allow me to show you." He unlatched the brass clasp, flipped open the flap of the folio, removed two copies of his book, handing one to Fanny and the other to Rose.

"The Book of Truths," Fanny muttered as she looked at the cover.

"I arrived with 200 hundred copies and intend to give all of them away. More than three quarters are already gone."

"What's your quest?" asked Ginny.

"The quest *is* giving them away. The trick is getting them into the right hands."

"Who are you giving them to?" asked Rose.

"Publishers mostly, but also a couple of book distributors and magazines."

"So you are trying to sell this book to a publisher?" asked Fanny.

"No, I'm giving it away."

"That doesn't make any sense," said Fanny. "People come to New York to sell books, not give them away. You're not looking to profit?"

"Not monetarily. I already have all the money I should ever need."

"Then what's the point?" said Fanny as she opened her copy of the book to its' first page.

"The point is to help people remember what they may have forgotten. The point is to show people that life does not have to be a complicated thing. The point is to remind people they are here primarily to learn and teach. Personally, for me the point is about giving more than taking."

"This is not true," Fanny said. "All things are not possible. I can name hundreds of impossible things."

"Yes," replied Herb. "I'm sure you can."

Fanny flipped to the center of the book and read out loud, "*Enjoying life is an acquired skill.* Well, here you are just stating the obvious."

Rose, also reading the book said, "*A bad friendship is like a toothache, it just keeps getting worse.*" She looked up from the book directly to Fanny, who didn't hear her or was ignoring what she said.

Fanny closed her book. "You want some truth? How about, the world is full of idiots. That's as true as anything I've seen in your book."

"Fanny," Rose scolded.

Fanny continued. "You want some advice Mr...?"

"Conroy," Herb replied.

"You better rethink these truths. The truth appears to have eluded you." She handed back the book.

Herb smiled and nodded giving reverence to Fanny's opinion, while Rose was quick to change the subject, "How elegant this place is."

Ginny took the queue "Yes, it certainly is that." The women chatted ambience and fashion while Herb, seated next to me, turned and said, "Bad advice is everywhere. Truth #13."

I leaned a little closer so only he could hear, and said, "Don't let Fanny's opinion carry any weight. I think your book is an interesting idea."

"I sensed you were going to get it. For some, it's beyond the range of their thought. How much have you read?"

"I must confess not much."

Herb's grin broke into toothy smile that stretched from cheek to cheek. "Then you haven't seen the last page?"

"No, only the first few. Why?"

Herb reached into his folio and took out another copy. "Something just happened here, I would like to bring to your attention." He handed me the book. "Go ahead and turn to the last page."

I did and read:

The book of truths was designed to be a tool. To use it, clear your mind and open to a random page. Don't be surprised if the truth seems relevant to something you are dealing with. If it seems irrelevant, clear your mind and turn to another page.

Feel free to add your own truths. Your own truths will help you understand who you are. Write them on the blank pages and pay special attention when your own truths appear.

"Why did you put this at the back of the book? These seem like important instructions to me."

"People should be familiar with these truths before they try to use the book as a tool. If you cannot accept these as true, then the tool will probably be as useless as a shovel to a surgeon performing open-heart surgery. Also, if you start out by randomly flipping pages, an important truth might slip away.

"Now," he continued, "back to my point. Do you remember the truth Fanny turned to randomly?"

"No," I had to confess.

"It said, *Enjoying life is an acquired skill.*"

"Okay, I remember."

"I would like to propose she turned to that page for a reason. I believe *that* truth is something she needs to learn."

"How so?" I said glancing at the women who were chatting feverishly about how everyone was dressed and paying little or no attention to Herb and I.

"Does Fanny seem to you to be enjoying her life?"

"I think Fanny takes pleasure from complaining."

"You see. There you have it. She could use that reminder to make her life better, but instead she is too preoccupied to see the truth even when it is printed on paper in front of her face."

"Yes, I see what you mean."

"Then what happened?"

I tried to remember but could not.

"What is Fanny's friend's name?"

"Rose."

"Thank you. Rose opened the book and read what?"

"Something about friendship?"

"Close. She read truth #30, *A bad friendship is like a toothache, it just keeps getting worse.* Do you think maybe the Book of Truths is trying to tell her something?"

"Yes. That's kind of amazing."

"I think Rose got the message. Did you see, she put her copy of the book in her purse."

"Does it always work like that?"

"No. I think the most important thing is to have no expectations and a clear and open mind. Give it a try."

I cleared my mind, opened to a page and read, *Truth #55 It is no accident that you are here.* I showed the page to Herb. "What do you suppose it means?"

"I don't know," he replied, "but I bet it's true."

Drinks were ordered, appetizers arrived and our feast was off to a running start.

"How many books have you given away?" I asked.

"I think I have about twenty left."

"Then will you be joining us tomorrow?

"No, I need to finish what I've started. But after that, I will be around so much, you may very well get sick of me."

"Will you print more of your books? Is this something you intend to continue to do?"

"Maybe. I don't know. In a way I'm testing a theory. I printed 200 copies with the intent of setting them free on the world. Whatever happens, happens. The people who find the book will either recognize the potential it holds or they won't. I guess I have faith the book will find its way into the hands of people who need it the most."

Small talk flittered about the table. Rose and Fanny told the group about their afternoon of shopping at Macy's. Rose thought it wonderful while Fanny did nothing but complain.

As we enjoyed our meal Rose said to Fanny, "Doesn't this place take you back."

"I'm not interested in going back. I'll take modern every time."

"Well, I love it. Thank you, Randy, for bringing us here and giving us this wonderful meal."

"Why are you thanking him?" asked Fanny. "If it wasn't for us taking his tour, he wouldn't even be here. He should be thanking us."

I was close to barring Fanny from future trips. "You are absolutely right." I lifted my glass. "Thank you, all of you, for taking our tour."

Ginny said, "It's been wonderful. I feel like I am in a dream."

Herb said, "Yes Randy, you've done an excellent job with this trip."

I looked at those eyes and said with a chuckle, "That's high praise from someone who has missed more than half of the tour."

"How true. Tell me, what have you folks been up to?"

"Oh, you missed so much," said Ginny. "We've been..."

Ginny and Rose informed Herb of all the happenings he had missed while Fanny poked and prodded at her food.

As dessert and coffee arrived, I looked at my watch and saw our timing working out well. "Is everyone as anxious as I am for the performance tonight?"

"Oh, yes," said Rose. "Julie Andrews, what a talent."

"When I was a young boy," I said, "Mary Poppins was released in theaters. I've had a crush on her ever since."

"You and every other man in the world," said Ginny. "My husband loved Julie Andrews."

"What's the show tonight?" asked Herb.

"Victor/Victoria." I said. "Starring Julie Andrews."

"I've heard she is having trouble with her voice," said Fanny. "I wouldn't expect much."

I was not the only one at the table tired of Fanny's comments. Ginny was now giving her the evil eye.

After our meal, outside on the street as the group and I waited for our van to arrive, Herb sauntered to my side. "Randy, I've had quite the exhausting day. I think I will make my way back to our hotel."

"Are you alright?" I asked.

"Fine, but all that excellent food has me sleepy. I want to be fresh tomorrow. I'm anticipating another big day. Am I correct our hotel is just a few blocks from here?"

"Six blocks," I replied.

"That's an easy walk. Could you point me in the right direction."

"No, I have a better idea. Why don't you ride with us to the theater, and then after we have been dropped off, I will have our driver take you back to the hotel."

"I don't want to impose."

"That would be the furthest thing from an imposition.   In fact, I insist."

At the theater, Julie Andrews surpassed expectations and gave a performance that left us loving her even more. Another full day completed. Three down, three to go.

Wednesday, December 11th, 1996

Truth #72
It is always a mistake to link money with happiness

Day four of our adventure took all of us but Herb Conroy away from Manhattan, upstate to the Vanderbilt Mansion and Franklin Roosevelt's home and resting place at Hyde Park. Our pleasant weather from the day before deserted us overnight and a front moved in bringing with it a humid cold that bit the skin and chased you toward shelter. Colorado's wintry cold usually lacks the humidity you find in East Coast winters. East Coast winters are sometimes punishing, and this day delivered a frigid blow.

At the Vanderbilt Mansion the driver took us through the main gate and dropped us at the impressive front door. The effect was to make the group feel as though they were arriving for a morning visit, not so much a tour. It being a Wednesday in December, there were no other tourists around. Other than a guide who met us in front of the house, there was no one else on the property.

It was a shame the weather had fallen inclement. The house is an amazing fifty-four rooms of opulence, but the grounds outside and the views of the Hudson River Valley leave no doubt as to why the very rich would want to have a home at this spot. Even so, this was considered a vacation residence by Frederic Vanderbilt, the owner and grandson of Cornelius "Commodore" Vanderbilt. As a family, the Vanderbilts were always trying to outdo each other for the biggest or the most outrageous homes. Many are now national landmarks or museums.

Inside, our guide moved us from one lavish room to the next, all the while talking about family history and how the

Vanderbilts acquired wealth through shipping and railroads. Frederick received a $10 million dollar inheritance when he turned 29 and was worth more than $70 million when he died in 1938. Most of the building is not open to the public, but what you do see leaves no doubt as to what it must have been like to be super rich in the early twentieth century.

After our tour of the mansion, it was time to find some lunch. In town, we pulled into a diner and split up amongst a few tables. I could have predicted that Ginny, Rose and Fanny would again end up eating with me. Ginny and Rose were fine. Fanny seemed hell-bent on fraying my nerves. At least today her breath was not as ripe as it had been before.

"I just can't get over all of the wonderful things we are seeing," said Rose. "That place was nothing less than amazing."

"Pure decadence," remarked Fanny. "No one should be allowed to live like that. It's obscene. It is just too much. It took sixty people to look after the house and grounds. The family was only here a few weeks every year."

"But that's a good thing," said Rose. They employed sixty people and those paychecks were spent here in the community."

"Oh come on, these people were the worst kind of snobs and thieves. They were ruthless and built their empires on the lives of common men. Don't forget, they called them Robber Barons."

"But didn't you hear our guide remark, Frederick was an unassuming man, not particularly taken by the trappings of his wealth?" said Rose.

"That's right," said Ginny. "He shied away from high society."

Fanny replied, "If you have a fifty-room mansion and you only use it two or three weeks a year, you've been spoiled by wealth."

"Fifty-four," said Ginny. "The guide said there are fifty-four rooms."

"Whatever," Fanny snarled.

"I wish Herb was here," Ginny said to me. "I would have liked to hear what he thought of the place."

"If you ask me that man is not well."

"Fanny!" Rose scolded.

"You heard him last night. Does anyone here besides me think he is more than a little bit strange?"

"No," Ginny and I said in unison.

"You don't think this "book" of his is a crazy idea?"

"No," we said again.

"What would you do with this book? Don't we all know what the truth is? I for one can recognize the truth when I see it. I didn't see much of it in his book. What is he trying to do?"

"Fanny!" Rose scolded again.

"You know, Herb has had quite the life," Ginny said. "Can you imagine, he's ninety-eight years old?"

Fanny cocked her head a bit and then exclaimed, "I don't believe it for a minute. The man is suffering from delusion. Something is wrong with him. He's living in a fantasy world."

"Fanny, stop it!"

"Something else, did any of you notice the way he smiles? He is always grinning. There is something not normal about that."

"How so?" I asked.

"It's just not normal. I've known some certifiably crazy people who smiled like he does."

I looked to Ginny. She looked to me. I think both of us were thinking something close to the same thing.

"I can assure you, Herb is not crazy," I replied.

"Don't you think it is at least a little bit strange that he would book a tour with you and then not do any touring? Why didn't he just come to New York on his own?"

I had to admit to myself, I wondered the same thing.

"I'm telling you," Fanny said, "I have had experience with people like this. I had a nephew who became schizophrenic. In the end, he killed himself. I'm telling you Herb Conroy is not normal. He's living some kind of fantasy. If I were you, I would be keeping an eye on him."

Ginny fired back, "I have seen nothing to lead me to believe he is imbalanced, confused, or living in any kind of a fantasy world."

"Do you believe he is ninety-eight?"

"Yes," she answered without hesitation. "Until I have reason to believe otherwise, I will believe him when he tells me he is."

"Fanny," I asked, "has Herb done something to make you feel this way?"

She paused then said, "It's a common symptom for people of age to lose sight of reality. I simply think the man has immersed himself in some kind of fantasy world."

Ginny said. "I don't think you know what you're talking about."

"So," I jumped in before the conversation could overheat, "Let's talk about what you are doing tonight. You have a choice of free time or attending the taping of a television show."

"I'm going to the taping," said Ginny.

"Rose?" I asked.

She looked to Fanny. "We have not decided. I guess I'll be doing whatever Fanny wants to do."

"I don't watch television. Maybe there is something else you could suggest?"

"The possibilities are broad. In Manhattan, you can experience just about anything. We could see if there are any concerts tonight. Do you like nightclubs? There is a piano bar not far from the hotel where the pianist performs nothing but songs from the 40's and 50's."

"Oh my, I want to do it all," said Ginny.

Fanny snarled, "I'm growing tired of music. Where could we find art? Not museums, I'm thinking painting and sculpture galleries."

"You could walk over to 57th Street. SoHo has some excellent galleries. Actually, there are galleries all over the city.

We should ask the concierge at the hotel. I'm sure she could suggest something to your liking."

"Would you be available to escort us?" asked Fanny.

"No," thank God, I thought as I continued, "I'm taking those who want to go to the television taping. If you don't come with us, then I'm afraid you are on your own."

Fanny gave an audible grunt of disapproval.

Traffic caught us on our way back to Manhattan. The jam set us behind a full hour. At one point, I began to worry we may become pressed for time, but traffic eased and shortly we arrived at the hotel.

Before anyone could get away, I took a quick poll to see who had what planned for the evening. Then Fanny and I had a talk with the concierge who recommended to her the galleries in SoHo. With that decision made, we turned from the concierge desk. Almost immediately, Fanny nudged me with a sharp elbow and said, "Now look at that man and tell me he is well."

"Who?"

"Just inside the door. Isn't that your Mr. Conroy?"

I had to look twice before I spotted him. This was not the same man who had started our tour. Having just entered, Herb made his way across the lobby toward the elevator with tiny, almost miniscule steps. The crowd in the lobby moved around him as if he were standing still.

"Maybe he is ninety-eight," said Fanny. "He certainly looks it today."

Herb's cane seemed essential. His feet shuffled with a short sliding motion as if to lift one foot in front of the other was not possible. If he looked tired the night before, today he appeared as frail as any ninety-eight year old might be. Abandoning Fanny, I weaved through people in the lobby and quickly moved to his side. "Can I help you, Herb?"

"Mr. Perkins, how nice it is to see you." He smiled an exhausted grin. "Would you take this?" He handed me his folio. "That would be a help."

I ran my hand under his forearm for support. "Tell you what, let's sit down and I will see if the hotel can lend me the use of a wheelchair." I steered him toward the nearest place to rest.

"Sitting for a moment or two would be good," he said. "But thank you, I will pass on the wheelchair."

We arrived at two richly padded, wingback chairs set against one wall of the lobby. A small table and lamp stood between. Herb removed his Landry hat and sat it on the table. He seemed relieved to be off his feet. "I don't mind telling you Herb, you don't look well. Would you like to see a doctor?"

"Oh no, I will be okay, Randy. I've just had more excitement than I am used to. It has been an eventful day."

"What happened?"

He leaned back and looked at me with an expression of pure disappointment. "I've made quite a mess of things," he said. Gone was any hint of a smile.

"Can you tell me about it?"

He nodded and paused, then said, "About two o'clock this afternoon, I found myself at the offices of Lucas & Loen - Publishing. I was down to the last three copies of my book. On the company directory, I found the name of the senior editor. I went up to his floor and was chatting with his receptionist, a young woman, twenty or so years old, cute. Anyway, we were talking about my book when her boss, a Mr. Mann, returned from lunch. He cast a questioning eye toward me as he walked past but said nothing to either of us. The young woman asked me to wait and followed him into his office. When she came back she said I should go right in.

"Mr. Mann's office is a big room at the corner of the building. Dark mahogany paneling, a wet bar, mahogany desk with oil paintings on the walls. 'Mr. Conroy, is there something I can do for you?' he asked. I took out the book and presented it to him. Over the course of fifteen minutes, I told him all about it, how to use it, the works. He thumbed through the pages, listened and was polite enough, but then abruptly moved

94

out from behind his desk and said, 'Thank you for this. We will keep it under consideration.' And with that he led me to the door and ushered me through. Back in the reception area the young woman sat up at her desk and asked, 'What did he say?' I told her and added that I thought he was trying to get rid of me. She said, 'You know, I've noticed he can be short with people. Maybe that's just his way? Did he keep your manuscript?' I told her yes. 'Well there you go. He wouldn't keep it if it were not under consideration.' She looked at me and gave me a smile that made me wish I could be twenty years old again. I thanked her for the help, but as I walked out of the office, I couldn't help but feel unenthused. Then, in the elevator on my way down to the lobby, I realized I left my cane leaning against the woman's desk. I rode back up and as I entered the hallway from the elevator, was confronted by the sound of shouts. It didn't take but a moment for me to realize it was Mr. Mann yelling at the young woman. I heard, 'WHERE DOES HUMAN RESOURCES FIND YOU PEOPLE? DO YOU HAVE A BRAIN IN YOUR HEAD OR ARE YOU PLANNING ON YOUR LOOKS CARRYING YOU THROUGH LIFE? COLLECT YOUR THINGS AND GET OUT.' 'But Mr. Mann,' she replied, 'he was just a nice, old man. He said he wanted to give you a gift. I couldn't turn him away.' I stood listening, unseen by the two of them. Mann yelled some more, 'AN IMPORTANT PART OF THIS JOB IS TO KEEP PEOPLE LIKE THAT OUT OF MY OFFICE, NOT RECOMMEND THEM FOR EDITORIAL REVIEW. THE MAN WAS A NUT. DID YOU EVEN LOOK AT THIS COLLECTION OF CRAP?' I peered around the corner and watched him toss the Book of Truths into the bottom of a wastebasket. 'IF THAT'S THE KIND OF SCREENING I CAN EXPECT FROM YOU, THEN YOU'RE USELESS TO ME. I WANT YOU OUT OF HERE. COLLECT YOUR THINGS AND GET OUT.' 'Mr. Mann,' She pleaded, 'I need this job. I won't let it happen again.' The man was unmoved. He stood over her, almost on top of her, yelling, 'YOU HAVE

TEN MINUTES TO BE GONE' That's when I came around the corner and startled both of them. "What's the mater with you," I said to Mann. "If you're looking for someone to be angry with, then bring your self over here." You should have seen the look on the man's face. Now mind you, he wasn't scared of me. He was probably worried I might have a heart attack or fall down and break a hip. Then he called security. I mean to tell you there was a time in my life when I would have followed him into that office and throttled him with my fist, not for throwing away the book, but for the way he treated that young woman. She had done nothing to deserve any of this."

"So what did you do?"

"I pulled the book out of the trash and put it back in my case, took my cane, looked at the woman and asked her to come with me. She said, 'No sir, I need to save my job. This paycheck is the only thing keeping me in college, and off the streets.' I felt terrible. Lower than low. This was all entirely my fault. How could I just leave her there? I couldn't. We both stood a bit confused, wondering what to do. Then a man in uniform showed up and politely asked us both to leave."

Herb sat up in his chair, looked around the room and then said, "You know, today's youth really have a way with words. She gave that guy a piece of her mind all the way down to the street. She may have uttered every expletive I have ever heard, and a few that were new to me. But the guard was very professional. He didn't touch either one of us. She was madder than a rattlesnake."

"So, you were shown out of the building."

"Yes. To put it politely, we were shown the front door. On the street we looked at each other confused and kind of bewildered. It all happened so fast. We looked around at all of the people. Then we looked back to each other and she asked, 'What am I going to do?'

Truth #6

Luck is sometimes disguised as misfortune

"I didn't know what to say to her. I told her I was sorry and how I felt completely responsible for the loss of her job. But she surprised me by saying, 'It's not you. This is typical of the way things work out for me.' Her eyes were as dry as a desert, but for her I wanted to cry buckets of tears. I told her I wanted to help. She said, 'I don't suppose you know where I can find a job?' I asked if she had any prospects. She took a deep breath, shrugged and said, 'Not at the moment. Both my tuition and rent are due at the end of the month. It could be a problem if I don't find something quick.' We talked some more and I learned she's a night student at Brooklyn College. She's doing it all on her own. No help from her parents. No help from anyone. We stood silent for a while. Then I asked her if I could have her address. 'No sir,' she said, 'I don't think that would be a good idea.' So, I reached into my pocket, took out every dime I had and forced it into her hand. It was $463 dollars. She looked at the money, and then at me, and back to it. 'Are you sure?' she asked. I insisted she take it and asked if there were some way I could get in touch with her. She again looked at the money, looked up and said, 'I suppose I could give you my cell phone number. Do you have a pen?'

"We parted, and I started walking. I thought I was walking toward our hotel, but I was not. I became preoccupied by what happened and what could be done to make it right. It was awhile before I realized I was going in the wrong direction. My mistake more than doubled my walk back to the hotel."

"Why didn't you take a cab?"

"I didn't have any money."

"You don't carry a charge card?"

"Taxi's take charge cards?"

"Sometimes they will take your jewelry if that is all you have."

"I didn't think about it. I kept walking and thinking and here I am."

We sat for a moment then Herb said, "Can I ask you a question?"

I nodded.

"I'll need an honest answer."

I nodded again.

"Do you think the Book of Truths is crazy nonsense?"

I shook my head and reaffirmed with a verbal, "No. It's different, but I don't believe it's crazy or nonsense."

"After today I'm beginning to wonder." He shifted his weight in the chair. "So now here I sit and the only thing I have accomplished is to cause an innocent young woman to lose her job. What seemed an easy experiment has now become a very complicated thing. I wish I knew what to do."

"Why not consult the book?" I said.

He looked at me considering, then shook his head. "No, I'm too wound up and exhausted. It wouldn't work. Maybe tomorrow if I can get some rest."

"Oh come on," I pressed him. "It seems to me this is precisely what the book is for."

He cocked his brow and then reached into his folio and took out a copy of the Book of Truths. He closed his eyes and let his fingers find a page. *Truth #94 It is hard to be friendly to someone with B.O.* He gave a somewhat exhausted chuckle and showed me what was written on the page. "I remember who inspired me to write that truth. Oh my. I hope I'm not stinking after my long walk."

I chuckled with him.

"Really," he said, "I hope I am not stinking."

"Not at all. You're fine."

98

"You see, to use the book that way requires a tender touch. I'm exhausted."

"Mind if I try?"

The brow lifted again. "Okay, why not?"

I cleared my mind, closed my eyes and opened to a random page. *Truth #24 Sometimes you might believe you have finished, when in fact you have only just begun.*

I showed it to Herb. "I'm not sure I like the sound of that." He squirmed a bit in his chair then said, "It has been a long, trying day. I should probably get going to my room."

I handed him his book and said, "Let me get a wheelchair."

"No. I don't need a wheelchair. We can go anytime."

Taking that as a queue, I stood and offered Herb my arm for support. He did not need it and rose without the aid of even his cane. "All I'm trying to do is pass along something helpful," he said. "It should not be this hard to give something away."

"Maybe it's hard for people to see the worth of something when it is free."

He cocked his brow and smiled, "Uh oh, now you've started to do it."

"Do what?"

"That was a truth if I've ever heard one."

"What?"

"You said, 'It's hard for people to see the worth of something when it's free.' If I wasn't so tired, I would write that one down. Remind me tomorrow."

"Can I walk you to your room?"

"You can ride with me in the elevator. People might talk if you walk me to my room."

His stride was much better as we moved to the elevator and stepped inside. "There is something I have been wondering about." I asked, "Why did you bother with taking our tour. You've missed most of what we came to do. Why not come to New York on your own?"

"I was about to when one of the staff at Seven Oaks, a nurse who keeps tabs on all of us, suggested I look into your company. Being ninety-eight, she didn't like the idea of me traveling alone in New York City. Your company came highly recommended. Believe me, I checked you out."

The elevator door opened to my floor first. Herb's room was another five floors up. I stepped out, turned back and asked, "Will you be joining us in the morning?"

As the door closed, he said, "If not, I will be sure to let you know."

I looked at my watch and suddenly realized I had just fifteen minutes before I was to be back in the lobby. In my room I brushed my teeth, splashed some water and dried my face, and was off again to meet my group.

Thursday, December 12th, 1996

Truth # 8
Giving is an art

Our last full day in Manhattan began at a leisurely pace. One couple got up early to try to be seen in the crowd outside one of the national good-morning shows, but after four jam-packed days and three active nights, most of my aged travelers welcomed the opportunity to sleep in.

Eight o'clock found me relaxing with a cup of coffee, reading the paper and occasionally watching the people in the building across the way. Some of them I had seen every day since my arrival. They were becoming familiar. I wondered if any of them had been watching me.

On my way to shower I noticed a folded piece of paper shoved under the bottom of the door. It was not there when I picked up the newspaper, which meant it had to have arrived within thirty minutes or so.

> "Good morning Mr. Perkins. I slept well, have had a good breakfast, and I am feeling better. Thank you for taking the time to chat with me yesterday. Once again, I am abandoning the group as I have realized there is something I must do. I see our itinerary calls for a ten AM departure, tomorrow. Unless I hear otherwise, I will assume this remains true. Until tomorrow, Herb Conroy."

Wondering what he might be up to, I put the note on the table, picked up the telephone and rang his room, but was not surprised when there was no answer. I decided to try again later in the afternoon.

In the lobby all the rest of my travelers were waiting. Ginny was quick to ask me about Herb. I explained he would not be with us again today. A bit dejected, she fell in with the rest of the group.

Our van took us ten blocks to Central Park for brunch at Tavern on the Green. There we were led through a twisting hallway to the Chestnut Room and were seated at a single table set for thirteen. Small talk encompassed much of the conversation. We discussed what had been favorite activities of the tour.

Rose said, "I don't think I could choose one favorite thing. Everything has been wonderful."

"Who is it that puts these tours together?" asked Fanny. "I have a few suggestions I would like to make."

"We have a tour planner in the office. All she does is plan our tours. Sometimes it amazes me how she fits everything together." Everyone but Fanny agreed it had been a well-planned tour.

"Randy, what happened with Herb yesterday?" asked Fanny. "He looked terrible. Was he all right?"

"What do mean, he looked terrible?" asked Ginny.

"Why, he came walking into the lobby looking every bit of ninety-eight years old. The man could hardly move."

Ginny cast a questioning eye to me.

"He's all right. He was the victim of a hard day and a long walk."

"Did anything come of his foolishness?" Fanny asked.

I let the question pass without a response.

"Are you sure he is all right?" asked Ginny.

"Yes," I reassured her, "He's fine."

After lunch there were three choices for everyone. I would make drops at the Metropolitan Museum of Art, the Empire State Building and for Rose and Fanny, more shopping on Fifth Avenue. The day sped by but thoughts of Herb often crept into my mind. Before leaving for our final show of the tour, I tried again to ring his room. When there was no answer, I left a message telling him his bag would need to be ready for the bellman tomorrow morning at nine o'clock, departure would be at ten.

Tonight's show was conveniently located just down the block from our hotel, close enough that I opted to walk the group. The temperature was cold, but it was only a half block walk. Before we knew it, we were seated and ready for the show.

THE KING AND I is a Broadway classic made famous by Yul Brynner years ago. Brynner put together, on both the stage and screen, a performance many believe to be perfection. Lou Diamond Phillips starred in this production and some of the group were skeptical he could carry it off. But in the end, performances were excellent from all the actors. All in all, it was an exceptional finale to our tour.

Back at the hotel I made sure everyone understood to have their bags ready for the bellman to pick up at nine, and at ten, to be in the lobby ready to leave the hotel. In my room, I found a blinking light signaling a message on the telephone.

"Hello Randy. Herb Conroy here. Could you please call me upon your return? Don't worry about the time. I will be waiting to hear from you in my room."

I punched in his room number and waited through two rings before Herb answered with a sleepy, "Hello?"

"Herb, this is Randy."

"Yes, Randy," he cleared his throat. "Thank you for returning my call. I was wondering if tomorrow morning you could join me for breakfast?"

"Is everything okay?"

"Oh yes, everything is fine. But if possible, I would like a few minutes of your time tomorrow morning."

"Okay."

"Can we meet in the hotel restaurant?" he asked.

"If you like. How about seven o'clock?"

"Thank you, Randy. See you then. Good night."

There came a click as he hung up his line.

Friday, December 13th, 1996

Truth #83
Superstition holds only the power you give it
If you give it power, it can be a very powerful thing

Departure days begin early for me. Whether coming or going, there is always a lot to do. At five o'clock, my alarm began to chime. By six forty-five, I had accomplished most of my tasks - my bag was packed, I called the airline to confirm our flight time, checked the group out of the hotel and paid our bill. At seven o'clock, I approached the hotel restaurant and found Herb seated in a chair just outside the entrance.

"Good morning Mr. Perkins." He said as he stood.

"I hope I have not kept you waiting," I replied.

"Not at all. You are right on time."

From the corner of my eye, on the far side of the lobby, I noticed a striking young black woman walking toward us. As I watched her I could not help but see, she also seemed to be looking at me.

"Are you hungry?" Herb asked.

"I certainly am. Shall we go in?"

"I've asked someone to join us. She should be here any time."

I continued to watch the woman move toward us until she stepped up and stopped at Herb's side. "Ah, Shauna, speak of an angel and there you are." He stepped back slightly to bring her front and center. "Randy, allow me to introduce Miss Shauna Jackson. I told you about Shauna. I caused her to lose her job the other day. Shauna, this is Mr. Randy Perkins."

I extended my hand. "You didn't mention Shauna was so lovely. Shauna, it's nice to meet you." I sensed apprehension as she shook my hand.

"Good news," Herb said, "Shauna has a job opportunity."

"Congratulations," I replied.

She sheepishly nodded and said, "It's not official yet."

"I'm hoping Shauna will consent to be my personal assistant."

"Your personal assistant?" I wondered if I heard correctly.

"Yes. Imagine that."

I looked to Shauna. She shifted, shrugged and said, "I'm not sure I am going to take the job."

I turned to Herb and asked, "What does your personal assistant do?"

Shauna answered, "He wants me to be his housekeeper."

Herb said, "Come now, you'll be much more than that. I'm anticipating something of an adventure. Anyway, let's not stand out here talking. If you two are even half as hungry as I am, then you are starving. Let's go in?"

A bit confused, I followed them into the restaurant where a hostess seated us and passed out menus. We had no more than sat down when Herb said, "Shauna and I had a busy day yesterday. We went apartment shopping and found a very nice place for me in Brooklyn."

I did a double take looking up from my menu and at the same time straightened in my chair. "You rented an apartment in Brooklyn?"

"Flatbush," Shauna corrected. "It's a nice place. Everything he needs is close-by."

"Indeed it is," said Herb. "The building is older than I am, but better maintained. I'm on the fourth floor, but there's an elevator. I wish you had time to come see it. It's furnished and ready for me to move in. This afternoon we are shopping for essentials - towels, kitchenware, and groceries. That is, if Shauna decides to help me settle in."

The waitress arrived and we ordered our meals; cereal and coffee for Shauna, French toast, scrambled eggs, sausage, maple syrup, a side of peanut butter and a large orange juice for Herb, an omelet and orange juice for me."

"Do you always eat that much for breakfast?" Shauna asked Herb.

"No, just on special days. This is my good luck meal." Herb winked at me and I remembered the significance of his order. It was the same meal he ordered the day he met Claire in the little café in Kansas City.

Shauna then looked to me and asked point blank, "Would you tell me if taking this job were a mistake?"

"I beg your pardon?"

Shauna paused as if recomposing the question, but before she could say anything, Herb said, "Shauna is wondering if I'm crazy, or maybe worse. As you know, she is not the first to ask that question. Can't say that I blame her. She has every right to be suspicious, seeing as how this all came to be. I am hoping you can be something of a character witness, Randy."

I looked at Shauna, and then to Herb, then back to Shauna again. She asked, "Is this man for real?"

I sat back in my chair, my mind trying to process the information, looked at Herb and said, "You're moving to Brooklyn?"

"Yes, I thought we established that."

"And you want Shauna to be your assistant?"

He nodded. "She would be good at it, don't you think?"

"I don't know. I don't know anything about her." I turned to Shauna and asked, "Do you have any experience with this sort of thing?"

"Taking care of someone? No, I've never taken care of anything larger than my cat."

I looked back at Herb, "You're not coming back with us?

Herb smiled and shook his head no. I could see he was taking pleasure from my surprise.

"Won't you be missed back in Denver?"

"I'm sure they will miss my checks at Seven Oaks. Otherwise, there is no one left to miss me. With the exception of you, all my friends are dead."

I was somewhat struck by the way he referred to me as a friend. It seemed as sincere as any statement could be. "But…"

"Yes?"

"I've never had anyone bail on me like this. What if someone asks about you? Surely, someone will want to know why you didn't come back."

"No one will ask. But if some one does, tell them the truth. I have always found it works best."

"But…" I looked at the two of them. "But…"

"It's okay, Randy. This is a good thing. "I've decided I'm not interested in waiting around for death's invitation. At Seven Oaks, all I have is a pleasant but depressing existence watching the people around me die. Well sir, I am not going to let that happen. With or without Shauna's help, as of today, I'm living in New York. What's the song say… 'If you can make it there, you can make it anywhere."

I could not believe my ears.

"You never answered my question," Shauna said to me.

"You mean is Herb crazy?" I looked to Herb and watched his grin break into an even bigger smile. "To tell you the truth I've only known him for five days." I looked into Herbs eyes. "Eccentric maybe, definitely not crazy. Tell me Herb, what are you going to do if she says no?"

"Well, I'm betting she will at least give it a try. But if she doesn't, I'm sure I can find someone interested in the job."

"What will you do on this adventure?"

"I am going to find a publisher for the Book of Truths. I expect that will take some time. I also hope to right the wrong I've done to Shauna. This is all happening for a reason. I could not be more sure of it if I had been granted a glimpse into the future."

"I wish I could be as sure," said Shauna as the food arrived.

As we ate, I said to Shauna, "Herb tells me you are a college student?"

She nodded and swallowed before answering, "I'm studying theater at Brooklyn College. I hope to have a career in acting."

Herb picked up, "Her classes are at night. She can help me during the day. This will be a good arrangement for both of us, don't you think?"

I didn't know what to think. Stunned was not quite what I was feeling -- shock -- no, more like a soft focus sense of bewilderment. Herb seemed more animated and alive than I had ever seen him. I looked to Shauna. With another spoonful of cereal in her mouth, she simply shrugged.

We chatted about a variety of things. Shauna talked about growing up in Minnesota and how all her family was still living in St. Paul. She asked questions about my job and the shows we attended. She had also recently seen the King and I. At the end of the meal, Herb sat up in his chair and said, "Well Shauna, what do you think? Are you willing to take a chance at assisting this crazy old man?"

She glanced to me out of the corner of her eye but never really broke eye contact with Herb. Confidently she replied, "As I see it, I have nothing to lose. Yes, I will give it a try."

"Wonderful," Herb reached into his pocket, removed ten dollars and his room key. "Here's your first task; would you be so kind as to take a bellman up to my room, collect my bag and make sure I didn't forget anything. It's packed and ready at the foot of the bed. I'll meet you in the lobby in a few minutes."

She pushed out her chair and stood from the table. "I think I can handle that. Mr. Perkins, if I don't see you again, it was nice to meet you." As she turned and left the room, I noticed many if not all of the men in the room, turn their heads and let their eyes bask in the pleasant sight of her youthful glide.

"You're sure about this?" I asked Herb.

"Yes. Absolutely. You know why? It's because of a truth I turned to yesterday morning when I opened the book just after waking up. It was, *Truth #26 Life is not fair or easy, but you can help yourself and everyone else by being fair and ever mindful of doing the right thing.* This is the right thing I'm doing. I'm so sure of it, I can feel it tingling in my body all the way to the tips of my fingernails."

The check arrived and Herb insisted on paying. As we moved out into the lobby, I pulled out a business card and forced it into his hand. "Will you please call me in a day or two?"

"Certainly. And next time you are in New York City, maybe you can find the time to visit me in Flatbush. You would be welcome any time."

"I mean it, you better call me. If I don't hear from you I am going to make a call to the police."

Our eyes locked and he extended his bony hand, and said, "Don't worry, you will be hearing from me."

We strolled into the lobby. Herb stopped as if remembering something and said, "Are you still interested in knowing why I believe I've lived so long?"

"Yes, absolutely."

His grin again widened and he looked at me with a lifted brow. "I always try to hold a smile both on my face and in my heart." His index finger lightly touched the center of my chest. "I believe it's my smile that kept me alive so long."

Just then Shauna arrived with a bellman pushing a cart that contained Herb's bag. Herb tipped his hat and said, "Randy, thank you for your help."

"Don't forget, I expect to be hearing from you in a day or two."

"I won't forget."

Shauna again said good-bye. Then Herb took Shauna's arm and said, "Are you ready? Here we go."

Somewhat dumbstruck, I watched as the two of them walked out the door.

Later that morning, as the group gathered to leave for the airport, Ginny asked where was Herb? I tried to explain but she looked at me as though I were an accomplice. She did not understand and how could she? Neither did I. I thought a lot about Herb on our flight back to Denver. From my carry-on bag I took out the Book of Truths, cleared my mind and turned to a page. It read: *Truth #73 What we know is forever eclipsed by what we don't.*

Seven years and five months later…

Tuesday, May 4th, 2004

Truth #101
Timing has a lot to do with everything

Not long after that December trip in 1996, I was promoted to a sales position at work. My touring days came to a sudden end, but on the upside, there was a nice increase in salary and the use of a company car. The job is somewhat boring but then, everything involves compromise. I often find myself longing for the excitement of travel. Some of the best times of my life were experienced on the road as a tour guide.

As for Herb Conroy, we stayed in touch sporadically, most consistently at Christmas when we exchanged letters and cards. As promised, a couple of days after our tour ended, he did call to say everything was good. He always asked that I come visit sometime. As it turned out, that was my last trip to New York City. On the rare occasions we spoke on the telephone, I could always hear the smile on his face and in his heart. He expressed frustration when I asked him if he was having any luck with publishing the Book of Truths. After awhile, I stopped asking.

Then while carrying out my work, a call was put through to my telephone. "This is Randy," I answered.

"Mr. Perkins?" a female voice asked.

"Yes."

"This is Shauna Jackson… Mr. Conroy's assistant."

Shauna did not have to say another word. I knew instantly from her tone that Herb Conroy was dead. "Yes, Shauna?"

"Mr. Perkins, I'm calling to tell you Mr. Conroy has passed away."

I should not have been surprised. After all, by then Herb was 106 years old. "I'm sorry to hear that, Shauna. I hope he went peacefully."

"Yes, very peacefully, in his sleep."

A dozen thoughts ran through my mind but mostly I felt a sense of regret. I regretted not knowing the man better. I regretted not visiting him in New York. An extended silence followed.

"Are you there, Mr. Perkins?"

"Yes of course. I'm sorry."

"Mr. Conroy slowed down noticeably a year or so ago. Last month, he refused to leave the apartment." I could hear a quiver of sorrow in Shauna's voice. "Six days ago, he would not get out of bed and early last Thursday morning, he peacefully passed." Shauna's quiver turned into a staccato weep as she tried to suppress her tears. "I tried to convince him to go to the hospital but he became angry whenever I brought it up. He made me promise I would not call an ambulance. All I could do was make him comfortable. Not calling for help was the hardest thing I have ever done."

"Shauna, I hope you know how lucky Herb was to have you."

"No sir, I was the lucky one. Mr. Conroy was like nobody I have ever known and I do not expect to meet anyone like him ever again. What I did for him will never come close to what he did for me. For the rest of my life, he will be forever missed."

"He was a special person."

"Yes, he certainly was that." I heard Shauna take a deep breath as if to compose herself. Then she said, "Mr. Conroy wanted you to have something."

"Really?"

"He wanted you to have his master copy of the Book of Truths. It's a hand written version in a leather loose-leaf binder. He was adamant that it should go to you."

I didn't know what to say.

"Mr. Conroy also asked me to do a few things for him. There is a storage container in Denver I want to look at. He was cremated and asked to have his ashes divided between a cemetery plot and a piece of land he used to own in a place called South Park. I'll be coming to Colorado. Would it be an imposition if I asked you for some help?"

"Of course not. I will help any way I can." My mind felt as though it were trudging through mud. There were a plethora of things I wanted to ask, and yet, I was having trouble organizing my thoughts. "When are you coming?" I asked.

"A week from Friday, if that's convenient."

"Yes, a week from Friday will be fine."

We discussed the details of everything Shauna needed to do and how I might help with accomplishing those things. After hanging up, I sat for a few minutes contemplating the conversation. I thought about Herb's life. I remembered his stories. I reminisced the details from that trip to New York City and tried to recall everything he had said and done. The day was long moments of memories and recollections. I went home early, as I could not seem to concentrate enough to get anything done.

Friday, May 14, 2004

The following week at 10 AM, I was at the airport waiting for Shauna Jackson at the luggage carousel. I scanned the face of every black woman I encountered and recognized her the instant I saw her coming my way. She had changed quite a bit from the nervous young woman I met so briefly that morning in December 1996, but she was still a beautifully attractive woman. Her shy demeanor was now replaced with an air of success. She looked confident and was smartly dressed. Under one arm she carried a purse and behind her, trailed a carry-on bag that rolled on wheels. I moved toward her and said, "Shauna?"

She smiled. "Mr. Perkins, it's been a long time but you look the same. I cannot thank you enough for meeting me here at the airport."

"My pleasure," I replied. "Is this all you have?"

"No, I also have a piece of checked luggage."

We collected her bag and then made our way to my car. The conversation was a bit awkward at first. I asked her about her flight. She said it was early and long and that it was impossible for her to sleep on the airplane. "Do you have a preference for what to do first?" I asked.

"Would it be possible for me to check into my hotel? I would like to freshen up and change my clothes."

"Certainly. Then maybe we can get some lunch before we go to the cemetery and the storage facility."

At the hotel, I waited in the lobby while Shauna freshened up and changed. She emerged from the elevator dressed casually in jeans and a pastel, v-neck cotton blouse. Behind her she trailed her carry-on suitcase.

To save time we grabbed some fast food and became better acquainted over burgers and shakes. With conversation, a little bit of time and some food, our comfort level increased and it was not long before we were talking as though we were old friends.

Our next stop was Fairmont Cemetery. One of Denver's oldest, it is a sprawling acreage with rows of headstones and crypts. "Do you have any idea where his plot is?" I asked as we entered the gate to the grounds.

"No idea," Shauna replied. "Our first stop should be at the office. I've been in touch with a man who said we could find him there."

I pulled the car into an empty space and parked. From her carry-on suitcase, which had been placed in the back seat, Shauna removed a brown plastic box. "Is that what I think it is?" I asked.

She nodded and said, "Half of him anyway."

Inside the office, behind a counter dividing the room, stood a thin, frail looking gentleman with gaunt cheeks and thinning hair. "Can I help you?"

Shauna stepped forward. "My name is Shauna Jackson. I spoke with a Mr. Gill last week on the telephone."

"Oh yes," replied the man, "I remember. I'm Frederick Gill. You're here to deliver cremated remains. Correct?"

Shauna nodded.

"What was the deceased's name?"

"Conroy. Herbert Conroy."

He dug through a basket of papers, "I know I have it here. I was working on this just last week. Oh yes, here it is, Herbert Conroy. We have a burial vault for cremated remains, grave preparation and internment of the remains. Can I have your urn?" Shauna handed him the brown plastic box. "Would you be interested in purchasing a more ornate urn?" the man asked.

Shauna said, "No, he left instructions that the box should be plain."

"Very well. As you know, most of this has been paid for by Mr. Conroy... oh my this says he purchased the plot and headstone in 1930. Is that correct?"

We both nodded.

"We don't see many people planning that far..." the man stopped and then said, "This is very unusual. Did you know this plot shows a mother and daughter are interred together in the same casket?"

Shauna and I looked at each other, both struck by the news.

"Did they die together?" the man asked.

"Yes," I replied. "They were killed in an accident."

"How tragic," Mr. Gill blandly stated in a matter-of-fact tone. He sidestepped and retrieved some of his papers, filled them out and then said, "Well, everything has been paid for but internment. I need you to sign here," he flipped to another page "and here." He reorganized his papers. "That will come to $189.65."

Shauna took out her credit card and paid the man."

"This will be taken care of Monday, or I'm sure no later than Tuesday unless weather gets in the way." He handed Shauna another piece of paper to sign and then her receipt. "Will you be present for the internment?"

Shauna looked at me and I shook my head. "No," she replied, "No one will be here."

Mr. Gill replied, "That will be perfectly fine." He took the brown plastic box and set it with the paperwork on a shelf at the back of the room.

"I'd like to see the plot. Could you tell us how to find it?" Shauna asked.

"Certainly. In fact, I will do better than that. The grounds can be very confusing. Why don't you follow me in my car."

After a short but winding drive following Mr. Gill's car, he pulled over, exited and waited for us to follow. We walked past a dozen or so headstones before he stopped and said, "Here you are."

In front of us stood a large, gray granite headstone. On the left side it read, *Herbert Conroy, born January 27, 1898*. On the right side of the stone, two angels were chiseled into the granite. The inscription read, "Claire Helen Conroy, mother, Born June 12, 1900, Died January 22, 1930" and below that "Lisa Jean Conroy, daughter, Born May 10, 1926, Died January 20, 1930. May mother and daughter rest in peace."

"It may take me a week or two to get the inscription completed for Mr. Conroy. Oh my, he was a centenarian. I will have to add him to our list. One hundred and six does not make him our longest-lived resident, but close. Our oldest is Mary Hatigun who, according to her headstone, lived to be one hundred and eight." After a moment, Mr. Gill said, "Well, I will leave you two alone."

"Is there anything else I need to do?" asked Shauna.

"Nope," said Mr. Gill. "You are all set." He tipped his head and said, "Good day."

We stood for a moment both having our own thoughts. Then Shauna asked, "Did you know Claire and Lisa were buried in the same casket?" She stepped up to the headstone and brushed some dust and leaves from off the top.

"No, I had no idea, but somehow it makes sense. Can you picture it, Claire holding Lisa, mother and daughter together for all time. "

We stood silent for a while. I don't know what Shauna was thinking but I was imagining a 32-year-old Herb Conroy, grief stricken at the funeral of his wife and little girl.

"He never got over losing them," said Shauna.

"Yes, but I'm not sure it was their deaths that bothered him so much as the circumstances surrounding it."

"You mean his leather case?"

I nodded, "Where is it?" I asked.

"It's mixed with his ashes. He made me promise to have it cremated with him."

I nodded again thinking that too made perfect sense.

She continued, "You know, Mr. Conroy used to sit and hold that thing for hours. There were times when he would sit all day with it in his lap."

We stayed for maybe an hour talking, before I looked at my watch and said, "I don't want to rush you, but we should probably get going."

We moved to the car and were then off for a visit to a storage facility. "Do you have any idea what we will find at this place?" I asked.

Shauna shrugged her shoulders. "I have no idea, but it cannot be much. The container is only five by five. Mr. Conroy hired someone to store all of his personal items after he came to New York City."

"Shauna, did you always call him Mr. Conroy?"

"Yes. I didn't feel comfortable calling him Herb. He was always Mr. Conroy to me."

It took an hour to find the storage facility; a large, secure, windowless warehouse surrounded by an imposing iron fence and out buildings made up rows of individual garages and rooms. In the office, we found a rather gruff, unshaven attendant who looked at Shauna's paperwork, checked her I.D. then said, "Have a seat. This one may take us a few minutes to find."

Nearly an hour passed before the man returned. "Come with me," he said. We followed him into the cavernous expanse of the warehouse. It reminded me of the final scene from the movie RAIDERS OF THE LOST ARK. There were rows of steel shelves with crates stacked almost to the ceiling. A forklift arrived and placed a wooden crate close to us on the concrete floor.

"We close at six o'clock," the attendant said as he handed me a key. "If you need more time, you will have to come back tomorrow." He turned and walked away.

121

"Very personable, isn't he?" I said to Shauna and handed her the key.

She shrugged it off, inserted the key, opened the lock and swung open a hinged door where something less than a dozen boxes were stacked neatly along with an old television set, three fishing poles, and a radio. The container was less than full. Shauna grabbed the first box, pulled it out and found it sealed with strapping tape. "I don't suppose you have a pocketknife?" she asked. I did and handed it to her. She cut the tape, opened the box and found unfolded clothes that had been crumpled up and sealed inside. "Wouldn't you think they could have at least folded these when they packed them?"

"Who?"

"Whoever it was who packed this stuff. They obviously did not care."

The next box we opened contained more clothing and a Landry hat. Shauna pulled it out, looked it over and then plopped it on my head. "Too bad it doesn't fit," she said. "You'd look good in a hat."

"Because I'm bald?"

"No, just because."

One by one we opened the boxes. There were a few kitchen utensils, shoes, a hand crafted quilt and two embroidered pillows. Next was a box filled with framed photos. "This must be Harry," said Shauna removing the top frame. I looked over her shoulder and agreed. In the photo, a young man stood dressed in fishing gear, a pole in one hand and his catch on a stringer in the other. In the background was a Nash pickup truck. Harry looked to be 18 to 20 years old. "Look at this," she said lifting the next picture from the box. It was Herb and Claire on vacation in Yosemite. From their clothes, the photo had to have been taken in the 1920s.

"How old do you think they were?" asked Shauna.

"I'd say 25."

"They don't look to me like people you would pair together. Is that a bad thing to say?"

I shrugged and said, "Opposites attract."

Shauna picked up the next frame. "Oh my," She said, "I was hoping there would be pictures of Claire and Lisa." In the photo, Claire was holding a newborn baby. It had to be Lisa because of the unusual point to her head.

"Did Herb tell you about Lisa?"

"Of course."

"I mean about how when she was born he thought she might be retarded because of the shape of her head?"

"No, " She looked closer at the photo. "But I see what you mean, she does look a little like a Conehead. Why on earth did he tell you about that?"

"Just about everything I know about Herb he told me during our four hour flight to New York City. In those hours, he spoke of growing up on a farm in Kansas. He told me about Claire and how they met."

Shauna gave a knowing nod.

"Ever since you called, I've been racking my brain trying to remember our conversations. Unfortunately, I think much of what he told me I've forgotten."

We took out the next photo. It was Harry, age nine or ten at some kind of picnic. Sitting on a patchy scrub of lawn, he had a plate with a steak in his lap. Off to the side you could see a dog eagerly waiting for scraps.

"This must have been taken in Dallas," I said. "Harry is still young."

"Do you know what Mr. Conroy's his favorite food was?"

I shook my head no.

"It was steak, just a bit on the bloody side of medium rare. He was a meat and potatoes man. Did you know that?"

I again shook my head no.

"His favorite dessert was warm cherry pie alamode."

"There are few things better than cherry pie."

She continued. "Did you know he was a bird lover?"

I nodded that I did.

"Not just any birds though."

"Ravens." I said.

"Then you know about Bonnie and Clyde."

I again nodded.

Shauna continued, "I bought him a pair of binoculars so he could watch for ravens out his window. Whenever he saw one, it seemed to make his day. He often took his binoculars with him when we walked. If there was a raven around, he had to stop to watch it. I always felt he wanted to follow them."

She reached for the next box and opened it up. This one was obviously older than the rest. Waxed and made of a stiff, thick cardboard, it had a lid that fit tightly and was not taped shut. Inside were three dresses, some children's clothes – little girl's, a doll and a shoebox filled with a collection of knickknacks, souvenirs, picture postcards, medals, a campaign button or two, award ribbons and lapel pins. Unlike the other box, the clothes in this one were neatly folded.

"Look at this," Shauna said as she picked up a round, white campaign button. In the center was a picture of the candidate and along the edge it read, 'For President Warren G. Harding.' "When was Harding President?"

"1920's." I reached in the box and took out a lapel pin that read Veteran WWI. "Did Herb ever talk to you about his military service?"

"No. I knew he was a veteran. He bought a flag to hang in the window on Memorial and Veteran's Day and the 4th of July. It was up for months after 9-11."

"That's right. You two were in Brooklyn."

Shauna nodded, "I was with Mr. Conroy. We watched it happen on TV."

"Can I ask, how did Herb react?"

Shauna thought for a moment and then said, "That morning was surreal. I honestly don't remember what we said. Mostly we were speechless, I think. I had looked at those buildings nearly every day for years. I knew people who worked in the towers and watching them fall was like watching friends die. Luckily, the people I knew escaped, but I didn't know it at the time. I went home and fell apart crying. But I do remember something Mr. Conroy said a day or two later. He said over his life he had learned that man possessed an unlimited capacity for both good and evil."

I wondered if that truth had made it into the book.

We examined more of the items from the shoebox. There were field day ribbons won by Harry in elementary school and picture postcards from places on both the east and west coast. A souvenir ceramic bell from Yellowstone, a fishing lure, three marbles, five Boy Scout merit badges, a small pocket knife, a baby's rattle, a black feather, and an envelope containing a lock of hair. It was obvious that every item in the box held a special memory for Herb. I put the items back and set the box aside.

I went on to the next box. Equally as old as the last, it had the same look and was also waxed. Inside, a set of bound notebooks, each one different but similar to the others, lay stacked one on top of the other. I picked the top one up, opened it to the first page and realized instantly I was looking at one of Claire's journals. Written in lavender ink with flowing strokes from a fountain pen, the first entry began:

Today I begin another new diary. This one makes number four. Herbert is away on business this week. I miss him, though he has been gone for only a day. The week will crawl by in his absence. I pray for his safe return. Fall is in the air. The weather is cold and gray. It did not warm enough to even dry clothes hung on the line. I am lonely and I wish Herbert were here to keep me warm. September 23, 1925

The next entry started below the last on the same page.

Today I made a Molasses Cake from a recipe in Good Housekeeping magazine. 1 good size cup of sugar, 3/4 cup of molasses, 3/4 cup of lard, 2 teaspoons cinnamon, 1 teaspoon ground cloves, 1/2 teaspoon ginger, 2 teacups cold coffee, flour to make a batter slightly thicker than a layer cake, sift a heaping teaspoon of baking soda through the flour, bake from 3/4 to one hour, in a moderate oven. It turned out rather well. I hope Herbert finds his way home early. September 26, 1925

"Do you know what these are?" I asked Shauna. She was looking at other items from the crate. "These are Claire's journals. I remember Herb talking about them." Shauna took one of the books from the box as I flipped the pages of the volume I held and let it fall open to another page.

Herbert and I are overjoyed by the prospect of being parents, but my morning sickness has become an ordeal for us both. Doctor Stikes says this is normal and with time will pass. I am now 12 weeks pregnant and have been sick nearly every day for a month and a half. My friend Mildred is a follower of the psychic Edgar Cayce. She says his cure for morning sickness involves mineral supplements and she is looking into what I might take. At this point, I would try just about anything. January 11, 1926

The next entry read;

Herbert brought home a new washing machine today. I wish he had not as the old one was more than fine. It cost us a fortune, $59 dollars, and is a modern mechanical marvel with an electric ringer powerful enough to ring water from a stone. I fear if I am not careful it could grab a finger or a hand and it might be powerful enough to pull all of me right through. Herbert says it will save time and that the old machine required too much effort, but I did not

126

mind cranking the handle to ring out the wash. He is ever so attentive and very worried about my health. I had the sickness again today, but it was not as bad as it has been. It could be the mineral pills Mildred brought me are working. January 14, 1926

"What are your plans for this stuff?" I asked.

Shauna looked up from one of Claire's journals and said, "I don't know. Storage is costing $80 a month. I would like to get it out of here, but I don't have room for it in New York." She put the volume down. "Do you want any of it?"

I hesitated for a moment and Shauna took that as a no.

She continued, "I feel like an important part of Mr. Conroy's life is in these boxes, but there doesn't appear to be anything of real value. I guess I will have it thrown away."

I live in a small condominium. Sometimes I feel like my possessions are pushing me out into the street. Despite this I said, "There is not much here. Let's load it in my car and I will take it home. Then we can decide if there is anything we want to keep."

Shauna smiled and seemed gratefully relieved.

We moved everything to my car. It all fit with room to spare. "Should we get some dinner?" I asked as we pulled out of the parking lot.

"Would you mind if I had you take me back to the hotel? I'm exhausted. I was up early this morning and with the time change and everything else, I think I am ready for some sleep."

"Certainly, I understand. We should talk about tomorrow. What time are we expected in the mountains?"

"Dr Ricksbauger is expecting us around eleven o'clock.

"Dr. Ricksbauger?"

"He's the man who owns Mr. Conroy's mountain property in South Park. He said, it should take about two hours to get there, depending on what part of town we leave from and traffic.

"Traffic shouldn't be a problem, tomorrow being Saturday. You have directions?"

Shauna pulled a piece of paper from her purse and we went over the instructions she had written. I had been to the area a number of times and did not anticipate any problems finding the place.

Back at the hotel, Shauna exited the car and retrieved her bag from the back seat. "What time will you pick me up tomorrow?" she asked.

"Shall we say nine o'clock?"

She thanked me for the day and said, "See you tomorrow at nine." I watched her enter the building before I exited the parking lot.

My drive home took only a few minutes. Once there, I unloaded Herb's belongings from the car and for lack of a better place, stacked them in my living room. After fixing something to eat, I settled in a chair, turned on the T.V. and searched for an interesting program. I must have a hundred channels to choose from but there was nothing that caught my eye. I turned off the set, got out of my chair, went to the box that contained Claire's journals, pulled one out and began to read.

Saturday, May 15, 2004

Truth # 10
Death is not a mystery
Death is a transition
The mystery is, where will you transcend?

I picked up Shauna at nine o'clock sharp. She was waiting just inside the lobby when I arrived and spotted my car as I pulled up to the hotel. As she came through the door she trailed her wheeled suitcase behind her. Dressed in jeans and a sweatshirt, with a light jacket draped over her arm, she looked ready for a day outdoors.

"Good morning," she said as she opened the door and deposited her carry-on bag onto the back seat, opened the zipper and removed a black leather binder from inside. "This," she said as she handed it to me over the back seat, "is Mr. Conroy's master copy of the Book of Truths. I'm sorry, I forgot to give it to you yesterday." I opened the cover and saw it was hand written - like the printed version, one truth to a page. Shauna closed the rear door, and then opened the front passenger side and slid in. I put the Book of Truths on the seat between us.

"Did you get a good night's sleep," I asked.

"Wonderful," she said. "Rested, fed and ready for a day in the mountains."

We headed west up Highway 285. Pleasant temperatures were forecast for all day. The sky was a bright blue with a few billowing clouds visible miles away along the eastern horizon.

Once in the mountains, the scent of pine lightly seasoned a gentle breeze.

We chatted about Colorado, the mountains, and how Shauna was strictly a city girl. Enamored by the scenery, she asked, "Do you think we will see any animals?"

"Maybe. It would not be unusual to see a deer or two."

"Colorado is certainly beautiful. I can see why Mr. Conroy would like it here. You know, he tolerated New York, but you didn't have to be a New Yorker to see that he didn't fit in. Sometimes I think the only reason he stayed was because of me. But here in these mountains, well, this is exactly the kind of place where I would expect him to be happy."

"Did he talk to you about Colorado?"

"Yes, sometimes. Mr. Conroy liked to talk and we talked about anything and everything. Mostly, he liked to discuss the events of the day. I learned early in our arrangement that conversation was something he expected from me."

"Shauna, do you mind if I ask about your arrangement?"

"What do you mean?"

"Tell me about your typical day?"

"A typical day... Well, I would show up every morning, usually around eight-thirty. Mr. Conroy would be up reading the paper or doing a crossword puzzle. Did you know he tried to do the puzzle in the New York Times every day? He never finished a single one I know of, but he tried to do it everyday. He said it kept his brain cells working."

"You saw him every day?"

"Usually. Our agreement was for five days a week. I didn't have to be there every day, but I worried about him if I didn't stop by to see him. It was no trouble. My apartment was only a couple of blocks away.

"He usually fixed his own breakfast, eggs and bacon, toast and juice. Sometimes he liked oatmeal, sometimes cold cereal. He had a thing for Frosted Flakes mixed with granola. If we went out for breakfast, he always ordered French toast and bacon, with peanut butter on the side. Course he also had to have his two teaspoons of honey every day."

"Orange juice?"

"Oh yes, had to have orange juice."

"Did you eat out often?"

"Not a lot, but some. Maybe a couple of times a month. Once a week I did the laundry. I was always cleaning or straightening up. Not that Mr. Conroy was messy, he wasn't, but sometimes he would leave his clothes laying around. I did all the shopping. When he needed something, he would send me out to get it. Sometimes, more so in the beginning, he would come with me, but most of the time, he was content to send me out alone. Not that he didn't go out. He walked the neighborhood almost every day. If he needed something, there were shops close by - a little market, a bakery and a butcher shop. It wasn't long before everyone in the neighborhood knew his name. Some of the kids started calling him Grandpa. He was a soft touch when it came to buying them ice cream.

"I helped him submit his book to publishers. At first he wanted to go to the publishers office, like he did at Lucas & Loen the day he got me fired. But I convinced him it would be better to submit the book by mail and wait for the publisher to request a meeting."

"Did that ever happen?"

"No, it never did."

"Did you think he was wasting his time?"

Shauna nodded, "Yes, I'm afraid so."

"Did you ever tell him?"

Shauna nodded again, took a deep breath and said, "I wish I had not because I think it hurt him to hear me say it. You know, all he ever wanted to do with that book was help people. He was convinced it held something. He said it was full of things people had forgotten. He didn't want any money for it. He wanted to give it away. But no one I ever knew could see the worth he placed on it. Not even me."

Something about the way she said that sent a shiver down my spine. "Did he show you how to use it?"

"You mean by holding a thought and turning to a page?"

"No," I shook my head. "You are supposed to clear your mind, not hold a thought."

Shauna slumped a bit in the seat as if deflated, "I wonder if that's why it never worked for me? Every time I tried to use it, I was doing it wrong."

Shauna reached down and picked up Herb's master copy of the book of Truths, randomly flipped to a page and read. *Truth #89 For pleasure, food and friends are an unbeatable combination.* She said, "I guess it doesn't work for me."

Miles passed in silent contemplation as Shauna and I became somewhat lost in thought. As we neared where I understood our turn should be, I kept a sharp eye looking left and before long it appeared. "How far did you say we are to follow this road?" I asked as I turned off the highway.

Shauna went to her purse for the paper with the instructions, "Three miles, always veering right until we get to a closed steel gate."

A ribbon of dusty dirt road took us through a stand of aspens that opened out to a broad field filled with sage and mountain grass. Just as described, we came to a closed steel gate with a cattle guard. I got out, unlatched the gate and swung it open, drove through, got out and closed the gate making sure it was latched. There were a few cows scattered across the landscape. The air carried the sound of an occasional "moo." We moved further down the road and as we crested a small rise, a house quite dramatically came into view. The place could only be described as a small mansion. A stone and log structure, two stories, but very tall, it was a harmony of angles with big windows and a wooden deck that wrapped around three quarters of the house. A four-rail log fence enclosed a perimeter of at least half an acre. Another cattle guard was set at an arched entrance to keep the cows away from the house. A hand carved placard, hung at the center of the arch, read, "Elk Springs Ranch Est. 1959."

"Wow," I said, "Dr. Ricksbauger must be doing very well."

Shauna agreed.

Once through the gate the wheels of my car met a paved driveway. I parked at a spot near the front door. As we exited the car, the front door of the house opened and out trotted a golden retriever ahead of a man dressed in a tan shirt and khaki pants. The retriever came to us in a welcoming jog, tail raised and wagging in a happy wave. I let her smell my hand and then scratched her behind the ears.

"Careful," said the man, "Bailey won't leave you alone if she decides to be your friend."

"Doctor Ricksbauger?" asked Shauna.

The man extended his hand to her, "Yes, and you would be Shauna Jackson." He turned to me and I introduced myself, also shaking his hand.

Doctor Ricksbauger stood six feet tall and wore a closely cropped beard rich with gray hair. Bushy brows topped hawkish eyes, a small nose and slanted lips. His body was of a fit man in his early sixties. He continued, "I am sorry we could not have met under more cheerful circumstances. Please, won't you come in?"

We entered the house and emerged into an entry that led to a large room with a spacious vaulted ceiling. The most striking feature of the room, a wall of tall windows, framed a view most easily described as breathtaking. A range of snowcapped mountains on the far side of the valley stood rough and rocky reaching thousands of feet above timberline. Below timberline, thick forests of pine blanketed the mountainside in layers of dark green. The valley of South Park lay below, reflecting lime-green hews of newly sprouted grass. Shauna, particularly struck, remarked, "I'm sure I've never seen anything quite like your view."

"Oh, thank you," came a female voice from behind. We turned and encountered a woman wiping her hands and smiling a welcoming expression.   About the same age as Dr. Ricksbauger, she was short, under five feet, with a round face and puffy cheeks, a small nose, no makeup on her face.

"Shauna, Randy, please allow me to introduce my wife, Ann."

"It's nice to meet both of you. Welcome to Elk Springs. I've taken the liberty of fixing a little lunch. Do you have time?"

I looked to Shauna and she replied for the both of us, "Yes, thank you. That would be nice."

Ann Ricksbauger led us through the kitchen to an informal, sunlit dinning table. The windows of this room also looked out on the expansive view. "This isn't going to be much, I hope you like turkey sandwiches and chips. I have water, ice tea, or a soft drink if you prefer."

"Or a hard drink," said Dr. Ricksbauger. "I would happily open the bar."

"Don't you think it is a bit early?" Ann scolded her husband.

"Just trying to be hospitable," he replied.

Shauna and I both opted for ice tea.

We sat around the table as she prepared four plates. Bailey, in the adjoining formal dinning room, stationed herself so she could watch and gave the impression she was not allowed in the kitchen.

"Thank you so much for allowing us to carry out Mr. Conroy's wishes," said Shauna.

"Not at all," said Dr. Ricksbauger, "You might like to know he made arrangements for this when he sold us the property."

"It has been so long," said Ann, "we thought he may have changed his mind. I never imagined he would live so long." She set plates down in front of Shauna and I, then went back to get two more. "Tell us, did he have all his faculties when he passed?"

"Yes," replied Shauna. "He was about as active and coherent as a person can be after a hundred and six years. Almost right up to the end."

"We feel very fortunate to have met him," said the doctor. "You know, he would not sell this place to just anyone."

"That's right," said Ann. "There were five or six people trying to buy the property. Mr. Conroy wanted to know what we were going to do with it. He was concerned someone might divide it to sell off as lots."

"There's one developer who is still after us to sell," the doctor continued.

"But we won't do it," said Ann. "That won't happen as long as we are alive."

The doctor bobbed his head in agreement.

Bailey patiently sat watching us from outside the room.

"What was here when Herb owned the land?" I asked.

"There was a small, barn-style cabin and a shed with enough room to park a car."

"It was a very nice little cabin," said Ann, "but we needed more space. Would you like to see some pictures? Let me get our picture book from the living room." She stood and went to retrieve a photo album. When she returned, she set it down between Shauna and I, and then talked over our shoulders as we looked at the book. The first page held pictures of Harry's cabin.

"You see here," the doctor leaned in from across the table and pointed to one of the prints, "Our house sits almost dead center on the spot where the old cabin stood. It's a near perfect place to build on the property, but we also put the house here because there was already a water well. Putting a well in these mountains can be an expensive endeavor, depending on how far you have to drill. We have an open, southern exposure that gives the building a lot of passive heat from the sun. For a place this large, our heating bills are next to nothing. "

"Not to mention the great view," I added and turned the book to the next page. These photos showed the demolition of

Harry's cabin. A bulldozer knocked it down. Then they excavated a walkout basement and built everything new from the ground up. Construction pictures filled the rest of the book. The last two pages were photos of the finished house. Nothing remained of Harry's cabin. There was literally not a trace.

"Is anything left from when Herb lived here?" I asked.

"No, not really," the doctor replied.

Shauna took her notebook from her purse and said, "Mr. Conroy asked that his ashes be spread at a place south from where Harry's cabin stood, in front of a stone platform overlooking the valley."

"She means the patio," said Ann.

Dr. Ricksbauger nodded his head.

"The patio?" I asked.

"That's what we call it. Someone, it must have been Mr. Conroy, built a terrace out of flat stones. There is a split pine bench to sit on. It's a wonderful place to look out across the valley. Sunsets take your breath away. After we eat, we can show you."

The Ricksbaugers were very pleasant and accommodating. They seemed genuinely interested in our lives and how we came to know Herb. After lunch, Shauna helped Ann clear the table. As the plates were being carried back into the kitchen, Bailey finally entered the room. I said to the doctor, "Bailey is very well behaved."

Ricksbauger, nodded, "We taught her when she was a puppy that when we are eating, she is not allowed to be in the room. There are few things as annoying as a begging dog, don't you agree?"

I nodded and remembered what Herb had said about pets being reflections of their owners.

The five of us, including Bailey, then went back to my car and retrieved Herb's remains from Shauna's suitcase. They were in a box identical to the one left at the cemetery the day before. Around the deck, we walked to the back of the house and descended a staircase to the level of the walkout basement.

"Did you design the house?" I asked the doctor.

"Oh no, we hired an architect who oversaw everything."

Ann said, "He came up and lived in Mr. Conroy's cabin for a couple of weeks, doing drawings and taking measurements."

Dr. Ricksbauger added, "He's also interested in buying the place."

Ann led us across the yard to a gate in the four-rail fence, lifted the latch and ushered us through. "Now if you follow this trail it will lead you to the patio. You can't miss it. Just follow the trail until it ends."

We thanked them and started down the path.

"Bailey, come here." Ann called, as the dog wanted to follow.

"Do you mind if she comes along?" I asked.

"If you like," replied the doctor. Bailey, as if understanding, trotted past and led the way with a wagging tail.

Before we disappeared in the trees, Ann called out, "No need to hurry. Take all day if you like. Let yourself in when you come back to the house."

Aspens and mountain grass dominated the hillside. In spots the grass was thick and on it's way to being tall. Bailey barked and chased a chipmunk as if clearing our path. About 300 yards, the trees opened to an overlook of the valley and a short distance further, the trail ended at a platform of flat stones and a split log bench. Aspen groves lined both right and left with the hillside descending steeply a thousand feet to the valley floor. A light breeze rustled the leaves and caused the grass to sway in rippling waves.

"This is perfect;" said Shauna. "My God, how could he not be happy here?" She turned a half circle taking everything in. "What's that?" she excitedly pointing to the left and down the mountainside. "Are those cows?"

I cupped my hands around my eyes to shield them from the sun, squinted and replied, "No, I believe that's a herd of elk." There were about thirty animals something less than a mile away. They were little more than moving dots on the landscape below.

I sat down on the bench. Shauna paced slowly back and forth looking at the landscape, trying to take everything in. We were quiet and just looked for what seemed to me to be quite awhile. Bailey sat next to me at the end of the bench, observing us as if she was curious about what we were doing.

"I feel like we should pray, do you mind?"

"Not at all," I bowed my head and waited for Shauna to begin. After a few moments of silence, I looked up.

"I'm not good at this. I don't know what to say."

"Why don't you come sit with me. I bet Herb would like it if we just reminisced. Can't you see him sitting up here surveying the terrain? I can. I can see him spending hours on this very spot."

Shauna came to the bench and sat.

"Herb was 98 when we first met him. Wouldn't you like to have known him when he was young?"

"Oh yes, very much."

"I think he was the oldest person who ever traveled with me on a tour. But you couldn't tell his age by looking at him. In fact, I remember thinking he might be lying about his age. So all through the trip I asked him, 'what's your secret Herb, your secret to longevity?' He had a bunch of them, but one he thought most important. He wouldn't tell me until that last morning. In fact, it was the same morning I met you. The last thing he said to me that day was, "It's my smile that kept me alive so long."

Shauna laughed a heartfelt chuckle and said. "You know, he was a smilin' fool. I don't mean that in a bad way. I mean, sometimes I would look at him and think, what the heck are you smiling about, fool. The weather could be bad or the electricity could go out or the toilet could overflow, but Mr. Conroy was always smiling."

"I think that's what I am going to take from Herb, the knowledge that it is always okay to smile, that smiling should be our most natural state."

"I don't know if I could do that. In New York, if you walk around smiling like Mr. Conroy, they think you are either crazy or stoned."

"Your turn."

"For a story?"

"Yep."

Shauna hesitated, looked at me with questioning eyes, then said, "I don't know what to say."

"Tell me about the best day you had with him."

She sat on her hands and let her lips widen with a huge, toothy smile. "That's easy," she said as her body rocked ever so slightly back and forth. "Almost every day was good, but my favorite was the day we celebrated his hundredth birthday. You know, he didn't like celebrating his birthday."

"Because of Claire and Lisa?"

"Yes, but I think also because of the way his mother died. I think Mr. Conroy thought his birthday was something of a jinx. That first year, the year he turned ninety-nine, I had only known him for a few weeks. The day passed without anyone but Mr. Conroy knowing it was his birthday. I felt bad about that. Then when I found out he was going to turn one hundred, I knew we had to do something special to celebrate. When I asked him what he wanted to do, his answer was always, 'have a good meal and go to bed early.' I said, 'no, no Mr. Conroy. If you don't think of something, I'm going to invite the whole building, no, the whole neighborhood, here to your apartment for a surprise party.' At the suggestion, I think I saw fear in his eyes and after a moment he said, 'Okay, lets go out to dinner. How about the Rainbow Room,' I could not believe my ears. Then he got up out of his chair, went into his bedroom, and when he came out, handed me a hundred dollar bill. 'Is this enough for you to get a new dress?' I thought, 'oh my God what's happening here.' Later I realized that I played right into his hands. He didn't want a party so he bought me off with a new dress and dinner at the Rainbow Room. He also made me promise there would be no surprises, presents, or celebrations involving anyone other than the two of us."

"Did you know he had been to the Rainbow Room?"

Shauna nodded, "He told me he had been there with your group. You have great taste when it comes to picking restaurants. That place is nice. I had never been there until then and it lived up to everything I'd heard.

Shauna continued. "The morning of Mr. Conroy's one hundredth birthday, I showed up at his place with presents. Besides his usual newspaper, I brought him a set of reproductions from the New York Times, all dated on his birthday in ten-year increments. One paper for every ten years of life from 1898 to 1998."

"Wow. I bet he loved that."

Shauna nodded. "He said it was one of the more thoughtful presents anyone had ever given him. I think he read every word of those papers at least twice. I also bought him a new shirt and tie. If I was going to look great for our dinner, then Mr. Conroy was also going to shine. I found the perfect dress - black satin with gold lamé accents, cut in a style that was similar to what women were wearing in the 1930's. That may be the best fitting dress I ever owned. But it was Mr. Conroy who had the biggest surprise. That night when I picked him up, I let myself into his apartment and found him waiting for me in the living room, dressed in a rented tuxedo, wearing my shirt and tie. You should have seen him. He looked like Maurice Chivalier or maybe Fred Astaire. He had on the shiniest shoes. Then he said something no other man has ever said to me. He said, 'Shauna, without a doubt, you are the most beautiful woman I have ever seen.'

I am sure Shauna was blushing but I could not see it because of the darkness of her skin.

She continued, "We took a taxi into the city. Mr. Conroy ate a steak just the way he liked it, a bit on the bloody side of

140

rare and tender enough to cut with a butter knife. I had salmon. All through the meal we talked about what he read in his newspapers. Then, about eight o'clock, the band started playing and people started dancing on that fancy parquet floor. I asked Mr. Conroy if he would like to dance, but he said no until a few songs later the band played, 'IT HAD TO BE YOU.' When he heard that song, he had me out of my seat and moving across that floor like we were dancing for a $50 prize. Mr, Conroy got a faraway look in his eyes. The way he held me I could tell that song meant something to him. When it was over, he walked me back to our table and he ordered a glass of whisky for himself, cake and ice cream for me.

"Herb was a lucky man to have you, Shauna."

"That's nice of you to say, but I was the lucky one. You know, Mr. Conroy paid for most of my college. He made sure I had health insurance and paid me a salary that was more than a living wage. If ever I needed a day or a week off, he never raised a fuss. I didn't know it at the time, but that day he walked into Mr. Mann's office and got me fired... that day turned out to be the luckiest day of my life."

Shauna took the box from her lap and opened the top. I witnessed a tear fall from her eye and land in the ash. She looked to me. "So how do you suppose we should we do this? I mean, should we put him all in one place or cast his ashes to the wind?"

I looked for a spot but nothing struck me as a good place. Why don't you spread him out over the area in front of the platform."

She looked at the box and wiped her eyes. "Could you do it?" she asked and held out the box.

I took the container, stood and walked a few steps off the platform. "What do you think, is right here good?"

Shauna nodded, and I began to shake out the fine gray ash. A light breeze suddenly surged and lifted some of the powder skyward. At that same moment, I heard a caw from off in the trees.

"Did you hear that?" Shauna asked.

"Yes," I replied looking around.

The call came again with three sharp caws. Shauna straightened and asked, "Is that a raven?" Bailey sensed our excitement as we scanned the sky and trees trying to spot the bird, but nothing was seen, and nothing more was heard.

With the box now nearly empty, I turned it upside down and heard a sharp 'clink' as a piece of metal hit the ground. A shinny glint of brass caught my eye, and I reached down to picked it up.

"What is it?" asked Shauna.

"I think it's a piece from the latch of Herb's folio," I showed it to her, and she agreed. Burnt and bent from heat, I rubbed the piece of brass in an attempt to make it shine. After a bit, I sat and put it down next to me on the bench.

"This is really none of my business, but can I ask about Herb's estate?"

Without hesitation, Shauna said, "I am Mr. Conroy's sole beneficiary. Except for the master copy of the Book of Truths, everything he had he left to me. He arranged his money in a trust that pays me monthly until I'm thirty-five. After that I gain full control over whatever's left."

"How old are you now?"

"I'm twenty-eight." Shauna hesitated and I waited as I could see she had something else to say. "I want you to know he never told me he intended to do this. Until after he died, I had no idea he left me anything in his will. In fact, he used to ask me if I was saving any money. He said I needed to be prepared to support myself after he was gone because all of his money was going to go to a charity. Shauna's tears returned. "I wish I could somehow thank him. I mean I hope he somehow knows. Do you think he knows?"

"Yes, I think he knows. In fact, I believe he might be here with us right now."

Shauna patted Bailey on the head. "I wish I had a camera," she said. "I would like to have a picture of this place."

"Maybe the Ricksbauger have one they can give you?"

"I wouldn't feel right about asking for one of their photos. I should have brought a camera. I don't know what I was thinking." Shauna stood, stretched and gazed out on the sweeping landscape. "Should we be going?"

I stood and looked with her at a sight I suspected I would never see again. Then we turned and let Bailey lead us up the path. About half way, I realized I left the little piece of brass from Herb's folio sitting on the bench. "Just a minute," I said to Shauna.

She stopped, turned and asked, "What's wrong?"

"I left behind that piece of brass on the bench. Do you mind if I take it?"

"No, I don't mind."

We walked back down the path and as the bench came into view, I spotted a huge raven standing with the piece of brass in its beak. "Well, I'll be," I muttered.

Shauna saw the bird at the same moment I did and said, "Do you think that could be Bonnie or Clyde?" She had no more than said it when a second bird landed next to the other on the bench. One bird passed the piece of brass to the other. Then Bailey saw them and began to bark. They took to wing with the piece of metal in one of the bird's beak. As they flew, the other called a chorus of caws.

"Now I've seen everything," I said.

Shauna replied, "Yes, I know what you mean."

The two birds flew south over the open valley. We stood and watched them until they could no longer be seen.

"That was a fitting end, don't you think?"

"Perfect," said Shauna, "simply perfect."

We walked back to the house with Bailey leading the way.

Wednesday, January 12, 2005

Truth #97
Some people do their best work while asleep

Eight months passed and over the course of that time, I thought a lot about Herb Conroy and the Book of Truths. His master copy Shauna had given me, I kept safely tucked away on a shelf, but the copy Herb gave me on our trip to New York City, I found a place for on a coffee table in my living room. I opened it often. Clearing my mind is always the hardest part of using the thing. But I must admit, the effect it's had has been helpful and pleasantly surprising for reminding me of the things I may have forgotten.

Before long, I started compiling my own set of truths. You can't avoid them once you start. If you know what to look for, you find them everywhere. As I noticed them, I wrote them down, as Herb advised, on the blank pages of the book. It wasn't long before I came to realize that the Book of Truths really can function as a tool.

Then last night, I went to bed and found myself seated at a table at the hotel bar in Manhattan where Herb and I had had our drink. Almost before I could wonder what I was doing there, the man himself came walking in. Under his arm, he held his leather folio. In his other hand, he carried his cane. His Landry hat sat slightly angled on his head and as he walked to my table, he was smiling. "How are you, Randy?" he asked.

"Good,' I replied. "What are we doing here?"

His grin broadened and he gave me a look I had seen from him at least one time before. A look that made you feel as though he knew a secret. Without answering my question, he asked, "May I join you?"

145

"Is Kentucky Bourbon still your drink of choice?" I tried to summon a server from across the room but he ignored me as if I wasn't there.

"Don't bother," Herb said, "He can't see us. Besides, it's impossible to get an edge on when you're dreaming."

"An edge?"

"You know, a buzz. You might as well be drinking water for all the good dream-drinking will do."

"I'm dreaming?" I asked.

"Must be. Remember, I'm dead." His smile broadened and didn't stop until it evolved into a beaming grin.

I expected to wake up. When I didn't, I asked, "What's it like?"

"Being dead? It's like being more alive than you have ever been, only you aren't." Through his smile, I sensed he was having a laugh on me.

"That's it. That's all you have to say?"

"Well it's different for everyone. A lot depends on what you expect. It will be different for you than it was for me. But I will tell you this, to rush the process is usually a mistake."

"What does that mean?"

"That means you should not be in a hurry to find out what it's like to be dead. Death is usually a sweet experience if you let it happen in its own time." He took off his hat and laid it with his cane on the table. "Now, our time is short so let's get to it, shall we?"

"Get to it?"

"Dreams have a tendency to end at the most inopportune times." He looked at me with the bright eyes of a ten year old and said, "I understand you've been using the Book of Truths."

"Yes. And thank you for that. It's a wonderful tool for greasing the mind."

"Ha," he chuckled. "That's one way of putting it. I'm glad." He leaned across the table and with a flexing finger, beckoned me to also lean in. "How would you like to do me a favor?" he asked.

146

"Certainly," I replied. "If I can."

"I want you to write our story."

"Our story?"

"Yes, our story of how you came upon the Book of Truths. Put it all down on paper just the way it happened. Then publish it and turn it loose on the world."

"What?"

"Write the story and combine it with The Book of Truths. Make it available. Give it a chance to take on a life of its own."

He looked at his watch, put his hat back on and stood from his chair, pushed it to the table's edge and said, "You will be waking up momentarily, and anyway, I have to go. Harry and I are fishing this morning and later Claire and Lisa will be joining us for a picnic lunch along the river at noon."

"You're with Harry, Claire and Lisa?"

He nodded. "Like I'm here with you now, I'm with whoever I want to be. That's one of the benefits. You'll see when it's your time." He reached out and shook my hand. It felt as bony as it had that first day at the airport in Denver. "Take care, Randy." He turned and in the blink of an eye, was gone.

I awoke from my dream and sat up in bed, as awake as any person could be. I went to my living room, found the Book of Truths, and opened it to a random page. *Truth #122 Every person's life is a work in progress, shaped every moment by the things they think, say, and do.* I went to my desk where the computer is always on, looked at the clock and saw it was half past four A.M. I launched the word processor and sat for a few moments staring at the cursor blinking on the blank page of the computer screen. Then, as if almost unstoppable, words came to mind and found their way to my fingers…

Sunday, December 8*th*, 1996

If you ever find yourself at Denver's airport around sunrise…

The Book of Truths

Truth #1

All things are possible

Truth #2

Risk should be measured by reward

Truth #3

Listening is an acquired skill

Truth #4

Change is inevitable

Truth #5

Unconventional thinking often brings solution to problems that elude conventional thought

Truth #6

Luck is sometimes disguised as misfortune

Truth #7

*For better health and appearance
smile*

Truth #8

Giving is an art

Truth #9

Great accomplishments are nearly always born from great risk

Truth #10

Death is not a mystery
Death is a transition
The mystery is, where will you transcend

Truth #11

Expect the unexpected

Truth #12

*It is not the amount of money you make
that makes the difference
It is what you do with the money you have*

Truth#13

Bad advice is everywhere

Truth #14

Eliminate the phrase
"I can't" from your vocabulary
and pretty soon you begin to realize
"you can"

Truth #15

We are all in this together

Truth#16

Happiness is not a birthright - it's a quest

Truth #17

*There will be days when it will take everything
you can muster,
to continue to carry on*

Truth #18

Smart people are not immune to making stupid decisions

Truth #19

To achieve most any goal, focus

Truth #20

People tend to complicate everything

Truth #21

To not try is a crime against one's self

Truth #22

At some point
the people who know right from wrong
usually wake up and take charge
Unfortunately, they often wake up late

Truth #23

Honesty is the base ingredient
of any masterpiece

Truth #24

Sometimes you might believe you have finished, when in fact, you have only just begun

Truth #25

*Put shit into your brain and before long, it
will start leaking out of your mouth*

Truth #26

Life is not fair or easy, but you can help yourself, and everyone else, by being fair and ever mindful of doing the right thing

Truth #27

Life is hard

Truth #28

Your past propels you into the present

Truth #29

*Racism is the bastard child of
ignorance and fear*

Truth #30

*A bad friendship is like a toothache
it just keeps getting worse*

Truth #31

One man's devil is another man's saint

Truth #32

*For achieving success
nothing beats hard work*

Truth #33

Without faith, there is no point to being

Truth #34

The best things in life are free

Truth #35

There is no such thing as a useless skill

Truth #36

Arrogance builds barriers to achieving goals

Truth #37

Responsibility is everyone's obligation

Truth #38

A wasted day is a missed opportunity

Truth #39

The key to success is never giving up

Truth #40

Some people are owned by their possessions

Truth #41

You don't always have to be right

Truth #42

Work should enhance your life

Truth #43

Life is an adventure

Truth #44

Not all sharks live in water

Truth #45

*Faith, hope, passion and conviction
contribute to every success*

Truth #46

Wishing by itself has never made a single dream come true

Truth #47

Life goes fast
Ask anyone who is old

Truth #48

*Any lie becomes believable
if it is told often enough*

Truth #49

The most important things in life
are not things

Truth #50

Wants are often confused with needs

Truth #51

*Lust has 20/20 vision
while love is stone cold blind*

Truth #52

*All the hopes, history, dreams, and
aspirations of humanity
ride on a speck of dust floating
in the immense vacuum that is space*

Truth #53

You are who your friends are
and the company you keep
plays a large role
in who you are
and what you become

Truth #54

Search for good in everyone
but realize, sometimes it isn't there

Truth #55

It is no accident that you are here

Truth #56

*You may never have a better friend
than your dog*

Truth #57

*Humility will serve you well in life
if you are smart enough
to keep some around*

Truth #58

*It's hard to hear what others are saying
when your voice is always
present in the room*

Truth #59

*Never underestimate your need for
friendship -- without it
you move through life alone*

Truth #60

Following your happiness provides the surest path to discovering your place in the world

Truth #61

Trapped people
have a tendency to be dangerous
Always allow room for escape

Truth #62

*Help people with needs
similar to your own
and your own needs
are likely to be satisfied.*

Truth #63

Just because you share the same space in time with someone, does not mean you inhabit the same universe

Truth #64

A person should never pass up an opportunity to laugh or smile

Truth #65

A person should never pass up the opportunity to make someone laugh or smile

Truth #66

Jealousy is a useless emotion

Truth #67

*Open minds have a
capacity for infinite expansion*

Truth #68

*It is possible to be alone in a room
full of people*

Truth #69

Opportunity is where you find it

Truth #70

*The boundaries you set
determine the scope of your experience*

Truth #71

If you don't pay attention, you won't know when it's your turn

Truth #72

It is always a mistake to link money and happiness

Truth #73

*What we know
is forever eclipsed
by what we don't*

Truth #74

*Knowing the past increases your chances
for being ready for the future*

Truth #75

Hate consumes reason

Truth #76

Enjoying life is an acquired skill

Truth #77

*Confronting fear is required
every time you try to achieve*

Truth #78

*A few deep breaths
can help settle an apprehensive soul*

Truth #79

*Lasting relationships survive
on healthy doses of compromise*

Truth #80

Success should be judged
by the price you have to pay for it

Truth #81

Humans hold an infinite capacity
for both good and evil

Truth #82

Only you can make your
dreams come true

Truth #83

Superstition holds only the power
you give it
If you give it power
it can be a very powerful thing

Truth #84

Perfection does not exist in the universe,
but to strive for it is a noble pursuit

Truth #85

*There are people who make sport out of sucking
the life from the people around them
In that respect, vampires do exist*

Truth #86

Imagination illuminates your mind to the infinite possibilities that surround you

Truth #87

Physically, you are what you eat

Truth #88

Attitude is everything

Truth #89

*For pleasure, food and friends are an
unbeatable combination*

Truth #90

*Focus on the beauty around you and the
ugliness will tend to disappear*

Truth #91

Peace-of-mind is priceless
To sacrifice it is a risky thing

Truth #92

*Music is a universal language
anyone can understand*

Truth #93

Everyone is brilliant at something

Truth #94

It is hard to be friendly to someone with B.O.

Truth #95

*Sometimes you have to retrace your steps
in order to find your way*

Truth #96

*You do not have to share the same DNA
to be family*

Truth #97

*Some people do their best work
while asleep*

Truth #98

We are all obligated to leave the world a better place than we found it

Truth #99

*Your brain may sometimes lie to you, but
your heart never will*

Truth #100

Common sense can take you a long way
Good luck if you don't have any

Truth #101

Timing has a lot to do with everything

Truth #102

People will find it hard to respect you
if you have no self-respect

Truth #103

Balance should be applied to most things

Truth #104

Trust is priceless, but earnable

Truth #105

Genius is born when insight collides with passion, dedication and conviction

Truth #106

Sometimes the only solution
is compromise

Truth #107

*Humans have two reasons for being
One is to learn and the other is to teach*

Truth #108

*We should all try to
give more than we take*

Truth #109

Every day is a unique opportunity

Truth #110

Positive thoughts
blazes trails for positive results

Truth #111

It's easy
and always wrong
to assume that everyone
thinks and feels the same as you

Truth #112

*Observation provides the opportunity to
learn without risk*

Truth #113

Bad days can be contagious

Truth #114

The ability to relax is essential

Truth #115

The harder you look for love
the less likely you are to find it
Relax and it will often come to you

Truth #116

Every moment holds the power to be
different from the last
The choice is yours

Truth #117

Helping others is often the surest way to help yourself

Truth #118

Know-it-alls seldom do

Truth #119

*Believe you can do something and you are
more than halfway there*

Truth #120

There is no such thing
as life without regret
Accept it
Learn from it
Move on

Truth #121

*If snow is available
and a boy sees a girl he likes,
he will almost always make a snowball
and throw it at her*

Truth #122

*Every person's life is a work in progress
shaped every moment by the things
they think, say and do*

Truth #123

*There are no limits
on the human imagination*

Truth #124

Good comes in all shapes and sizes
Unfortunately, evil possesses the same trait

Truth #125

*In every life there are days of great joy
and days of great sorrow*

Truth #126

*Ideas are the seeds from which
everything is born*

Truth #127

*Words should be at least
slightly thought about
before they exit one's mouth*

Truth #128

Friends should be chosen carefully

Truth #129

*It is hard for people to see the worth of
something when it is free*

Truth #130

Everything is born from thought
Every thing

Truth #131

*Embrace your fear and it will
easier to conquer*

Truth #132

*Your deeds are the paint you use to color
the canvas that is your life*

*Rosy pictures are not required
or even preferred*

Truth #133

Hope was the spark that ignited creation

Truth #134

There is no failure in making a mistake
Failure comes when you make
the same mistake more than once

Truth #135

*In the end
all that is left is the memory
of what you were*

The Book of Truths was designed to be a tool. To use it, clear your mind and open to a random page. Don't be surprised if the truth seems relevant to something you are dealing with. If it seems irrelevant, clear your mind and turn to another page.

Feel free to add your own truths. Your own truths will show you who you are. Write them on the blank pages and pay special attention when your own truths appear.